"Ross, I Won't Argue with You. I Must Go,"

she finished desperately.

Quickly she ran from the car. Despite the rain and the tears that blinded her eyes, she made her way to the front door. But as she was about to step across the threshold, into warmth and safety, she stopped.

Powerful emotions raged within her. She was torn between her desire for this man and her freedom.

Love won.

Slowly she turned and a dark figure came toward her. He stopped only inches away.

"Surrender," he urged huskily. "Even the walls of this castle couldn't keep me from you tonight."

PAMELA WALLACE
is a professional writer who has written for TV and magazines, as well as numerous works of fiction. Her spirited characters come alive on every page as she weaves a thought-provoking story of true-to-life romance. Ms. Wallace lives in Fresno, California.

Dear Reader:

Silhouette has always tried to give you exactly what you want. When you asked for increased realism, deeper characterization and greater length, we brought you Silhouette Special Editions. When you asked for increased sensuality, we brought you Silhouette Desire. Now you ask for books with the length and depth of Special Editions, the sensuality of Desire, but with something else besides, something that no one else offers. Now we bring you SILHOUETTE INTIMATE MOMENTS, true romance novels, longer than the usual, with all the depth that length requires. More sensuous than the usual, with characters whose maturity matches that sensuality. Books with the ingredient no one else has tapped: excitement.

There is an electricity between two people in love that makes everything they do magic, larger than life—and this is what we bring you in SILHOUETTE INTIMATE MOMENTS. Look for them wherever you buy books.

These books are for the woman who wants more than she has ever had before. These books are for you. As always, we look forward to your comments and suggestions. You can write to me at the address below:

Karen Solem
Editor-in-Chief
Silhouette Books
P.O. Box 769
New York, N.Y. 10019

PAMELA WALLACE
Dreams Lost, Dreams Found

Silhouette Special Edition
Published by Silhouette Books New York
America's Publisher of Contemporary Romance

Other Silhouette Books by Pamela Wallace

Come Back, My Love
Love with a Perfect Stranger

 SILHOUETTE BOOKS, a Simon & Schuster Division of
GULF & WESTERN CORPORATION
1230 Avenue of the Americas, New York, N.Y. 10020

Copyright © 1983 by Pamela Wallace

Distributed by Pocket Books

ISBN: 0-671-53602-8

First Silhouette Books printing June, 1983

10 9 8 7 6 5 4 3 2 1

Map by Ray Lundgren

SILHOUETTE, SILHOUETTE SPECIAL EDITION and
colophon are registered trademarks of Simon & Schuster.

America's Publisher of Contemporary Romance

Printed in the U.S.A.

Laurie's Lament

On my garden wall,
  moonlight traces patterns
  of yesterday's sweet bouquet.
Then, genestra, satin-glossed and yellow-bright,
  swayed on slender stems and danced partners
  with a gentle wind.
Now, in this quiet night,
  my heart calls
  to yesterday when love was—
  and shadows did not pattern
  on my garden wall.

—Elnora King

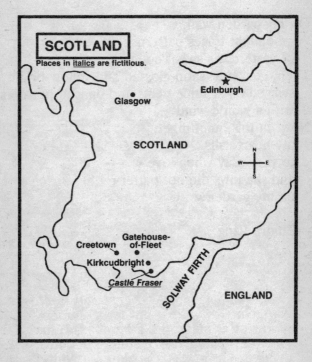

SCOTLAND

Places in _italics_ are fictitious.

Glasgow

Edinburgh

SCOTLAND

N
W   E
S

Creetown

Gatehouse-
of-Fleet

Kirkcudbright

Castle Fraser

SOLWAY FIRTH

ENGLAND

Chapter One

Brynne McAllister locked the door behind her, then turned and headed down the brick path to her front gate. The gate was old and rickety, the wood splintered, but Brynne refused to have it replaced. It had charm and character, like her Cape Cod–style white-shuttered cottage. As Brynne unlatched the gate, her eye was caught for a moment by the profusion of color in her front yard: luxuriant vines of fuchsia, tall bushes of heliotrope, and masses of brightly colored wildflowers—poppies, lupines, and wild pansies.

Flowers always seemed to bloom in Carmel, but in the spring they were especially luxuriant. Now, in early April, they were a riot of color.

Spring is definitely here, Brynne thought as

she set off down the steep, winding road that led to the business district of Carmel. The sky was a brilliant blue, and the sun was already warm. Brynne realized with a small rueful smile that she didn't need the mint-green cashmere sweater she had carelessly thrown over a matching silk blouse.

There was a sense of change in the warm spring air, a mood of expectancy. It affected Brynne profoundly, making her glow with excitement. At thirty-one, she was a lovely woman whose beauty was in full bloom. Her luminous topaz eyes, a tawny golden brown, contrasted vividly with the pale cream of her complexion. The morning light caught red-gold highlights in her strawberry-blond hair that fell, baby-fine and straight, past her shoulders. She was of medium height, her body all soft curves and fullness in just the right places.

After a sad and dreary winter, Brynne found this spring exhilarating. She hummed as she walked along, something she hadn't done in months. She felt happy and light-hearted for no particular reason.

At the bottom of the hill, where San Antonio Road met Ocean Avenue, the main street of Carmel, Brynne stopped to watch the ocean, only a hundred yards away. On this clear, bright morning, the sea was a translucent aquamarine. As Brynne watched, a wave swept up on the wide expanse of sandy beach with a powerful surge. As always, the ocean's endless horizon gave her a feeling of freedom, of limitless possibilities. . . .

"Brynne, love, good morning to you!"

Startled out of her reverie, Brynne turned to see Jason Klein jogging toward her. Rich and eccentric, he was dressed, as usual, flamboyantly, in a mauve velour jogging suit. His black hair, thinning on top, was carefully combed and sprayed to cover his bald spot. Brynne couldn't help smiling at Jason's vanity. But though she often thought him silly, she was very fond of him.

He was about fifty, though he was vague about his exact age. He carefully cultivated the image of the roving bachelor. However much he flirted with her, Brynne knew that he was, at heart, a good friend. He had been close to Brynne's family since they'd moved to Carmel fifteen years earlier.

"Good morning, Jason," Brynne said with real warmth in her voice. "It's a beautiful day, isn't it?"

"It is, indeed." His black eyes looked at her shrewdly, then he continued easily, "You're looking especially chipper today."

"It's spring, the weather's gorgeous."

"It is definitely spring, a time of new beginnings," Jason responded meaningfully. Then, as if suddenly coming to a decision, he went on quickly, "Come with me to my car. It's parked just over there. I've got something for you."

"What?"

"You'll see. I've been keeping it in my glove compartment for some time, waiting for just the right moment to give it to you. I think now is the time."

His car, an expensive bright red Ferrari, was parked on Ocean Avenue, just a few yards away. As he unlocked it and reached into the glove compartment, he explained, "I've been watching you all winter for signs that you were coming to life again after Allen's death. Just lately, I've sensed a different mood in you."

Allen . . . For a moment Brynne felt the familiar pang of sadness for the loss of her husband. But this time she also felt guilty, for she hadn't thought of him at all this morning.

Jason handed Brynne a brown paper bag.

"What's this—last week's ham-and-cheese?" Brynne asked, trying to sound light and flip.

But as she opened the bag, she found another bag, made of golden-brown velvet, with a moss-green velvet ribbon running through a top hem. As Brynne untied the ribbon and loosened the drawstring, she knew Jason was watching her intently.

"For heaven's sake, hurry up, young lady. I need to get home to my breakfast of sunflower seeds and yogurt."

Smiling at Jason's self-mocking tone, Brynne drew out a small pair of sterling-silver-handled scissors fastened to the inside of the velvet bag with a black silk cord.

"There's room enough for you to cut the cord with the scissors. Think of that cord as a tie to grief. It's been one year since you lost Allen, Brynne. It's time to put yesterday behind you and get on with life."

Brynne's smile had faded as Jason softly spoke to her. There was a lump in her throat, and she couldn't speak.

"Allen loved life and he loved being with

you. But he's gone now. You've mourned long enough. Cut, snip, sever . . . but embrace life again, my dear."

Brynne had tears in her eyes as she kissed Jason affectionately on the cheek. Then, as she looked down at the scissors that were so symbolic, a kaleidoscope of scenes flashed through her mind: the first time she and Allen made love—he was so infinitely tender with her that for the first time she realized how truly intimate lovemaking could be . . . Allen laughing, playing with her, teasing her . . . the portrait he painted of her, the one painting he always refused to sell . . . and finally, Allen's body lying lifeless in the hospital emergency room, all that vitality and love and energy suddenly drained from it.

Brynne hesitated no longer. She cut the cord at its knot.

Looking up at Jason, she said softly, "Thank you. This day seemed different from the start. And now I know why."

"You're quite welcome, my dear child. Well, I'm off. See you around."

He jogged away in his funny stiff-kneed way.

Brynne continued standing there watching the ocean for some time.

Freedom . . . For the first time in my life, I'm entirely free, she thought. I'm no one's daughter, no one's wife. I belong only to myself. And that knowledge isn't entirely frightening. I can do what I please, have an adventure, indulge a whim.

She realized that Jason was right when he implied the healing process had been going on for months, since Allen's death last spring. It was only now that she was aware of it.

As she turned and headed up the tree-shaded esplanade that ran down the center of Ocean Avenue, she thought with a sense of wonder of the healing powers of time. Only one year ago, as she stood by Allen's grave, she had thought her life was over. Now she realized that it was simply entering a new phase.

As she walked, Brynne looked around curiously, as if she were seeing the world for the first time. The quaint village of Carmel, on the coast south of San Francisco, was tucked away beneath magnificent pines, oaks, and eucalypti. It doubled back and forth over a hill whose roads wound around steep canyons. Brynne took it all in—the pine-clad hills, the crescent-shaped beach, windswept cypress trees, and blue bay. In the distance, mountains rose in wavelike layers.

The town itself was as lovely as the locale. It was small, only one square mile, a few thousand inhabitants. The buildings were a charming mishmash of styles—Spanish, Mediterranean, ultramodern, colonial, all standing side by side. After the San Francisco earthquake and fire in 1906, bohemian artists, writers, and poets who were burned out of the city opened studios in Carmel and stayed on. They attracted others of the same type, artists looking for natural beauty, craftsmen, writers. These people gave Carmel its atmosphere of free-wheeling individualism and nonconformity.

Brynne turned off Ocean Avenue onto one of

the many tiny, winding side streets that branched off it. A moment later she was unlocking the door of the McAllister Gallery. She loved this time of day best—just before she opened for business, when all was quiet and serene. She was alone with the paintings she had selected so carefully.

Her mother, Rachel, had bought this gallery fifteen years earlier, following the death of Brynne's father in Vietnam. After their nomadic life in the army, and more moves than she could count on both hands, Rachel was determined to put down roots somewhere. She chose Carmel because of her interest in art and because she thought her two daughters, Brynne, then sixteen, and Jane, ten, would be happy there.

Brynne often wondered what her mother was like before she became an army wife and mother. She was a remarkable woman in many ways. At seventeen she had left her parents' small farm in Northern California to study art in San Francisco. Her stern, old-world parents strongly disapproved of their only child's ambitions, and cut her off without either emotional or financial support. She was on her own. But she always told Brynne that she was never afraid. Living in San Francisco was fun, even on a shoestring budget, and she was confident of her talent as an artist.

Then one night she met Andrew McAllister, a dashing young lieutenant based at the Presidio. He had a three-day leave, and before it was over he had persuaded Rachel to marry him.

Her independence, and her art career, were

left behind as she followed her husband
around the world. A devoted, happy wife and
mother, she never seemed to regret her decision. "We all have to make choices in life,"
she once told Brynne. "I'm happy with the
choices I've made."

Brynne understood that. She'd had her own
choices to make, too. When her mother died
only three years after coming to Carmel,
Jason Klein had offered to buy the gallery.
Instead, Brynne had left college, putting
aside her own artistic aspirations to run the
gallery herself and raise Jane. At first she was
terrified, unsure of her ability to handle such
responsibility. It was Jason who gave her the
courage to get past the awful beginning.

"If you're determined to do this, do it right.
Put away your jeans and T-shirts and put on
something silk and expensive," he told her as
she sat forlornly in the gallery on the day after
her mother's funeral. "Wear dangly gold earrings, develop an 'arty' look. If you're going to
be a gallery owner, you must look the part.
And I'll be around, love, whenever you need
help."

And he was. Soon Brynne was too busy
learning what she had to learn, to be scared.
And after a while, she was no longer scared at
all.

Then, when Jane went off to college,
Brynne met Allen. He was talented but broke.
It was logical that Brynne would continue
running the gallery, supporting them. She
kept her maiden name in business dealings,
but in private she was Mrs. Hunter.

Someday, Brynne had always thought,

there would be time for her. Over the years, Allen had become more and more successful. His last show had attracted attention from some influential people in the art world. His prices rose, and for the first time he was in a position to support Brynne.

Then, when everything looked most hopeful, Allen died unexpectedly of an aneurysm.

Thinking about Allen now, Brynne realized that everything happened quickly with him—falling in love, getting married, becoming successful, even dying. It was like the watercolors he painted. He did them in a rapid burst of movement, for once the wash was applied, the painting had to be finished quickly.

His lovely pastel watercolors filled the gallery now. He'd been working hard, producing a great deal just before he died. With the ultimate irony that affects most artists, his work was worth a great deal more when he was dead than when he was alive.

As Brynne thought of Allen, she moved about the gallery straightening pictures, dusting tables. She was glad she could remember him now calmly, without having to fight back tears and a terrifying sense of loss.

Jason was right, she thought as she unlocked the doors precisely at nine o'clock. It's time to get on with life, time to do something different, something just for me.

But what? she wondered as the first customers came in.

Brynne was sitting in front of the fire in her living room, leafing through a magazine, when the idea struck her. It was a pleasant,

cozy room. The windows were covered by
filmy white priscilla curtains. Shaggy white
area rugs were scattered over the gleaming
hardwood floor. Lush green plants were
everywhere, hanging from the ceiling, sitting
in blue-and-white porcelain bowls on occa-
sional tables. The wallpaper was a design of
tiny blue flowers against a white background.
The same design was repeated in the sofa and
armchairs that stood by the small white-
manteled fireplace.

Nights were chilly in Carmel, even in the
spring, and Brynne was grateful for the
warmth of the brightly crackling fire. She was
curled up in a corner of the sofa, with a glass
of wine on the small oak coffee table in front
of her. Outside, a gentle spring rain was falling, pattering lightly against the windows.
The room was in semidarkness broken only by
the dancing firelight and the light from a
single lamp just behind Brynne.

The magazine she was reading was filled
with fashions and advertisements. Brynne
was only half-looking at it as she thumbed
through the glossy pages. Then suddenly her
eye was caught by a small picture. It was a
castle, and the caption below read, "Castle
Fraser, Kirkcudbright, Scotland."

Holding the page closer, Brynne stared at
the picture. The castle looked old and run-
down, and the stone walls surrounding it were
covered with untamed ivy. Yet it intrigued
Brynne somehow. She read the copy and discovered the castle was for sale, for only
$125,000.

She looked once more at the picture. It was

the kind of castle that fairy tales are made of, with turrets and archways, and a cobbled courtyard. Inexplicably, Brynne felt drawn to the place. It was enchanting, a charming anachronism in a world grown too coldly modern.

Then, too, Brynne's heritage on her father's side was Scottish. Her great-grandfather had come from the slums of Glasgow to the promised land of America before the turn of the century. He was still alive when Brynne was small and he had told her tales of the old country. This early influence had led Brynne later to read Sir Walter Scott's romantic stories of Scotland. She had always thought that someday she would travel to Scotland, to get in touch with her heritage.

Now, as Brynne looked at the picture of Castle Fraser, she felt her Scots blood stir.

Once more Brynne looked at the price: $125,000. A small sum, really, for a romantic piece of history. But a fortune if you didn't have it. And Brynne didn't have it. She made a good living with the gallery, but not nearly *that* good.

Kirkcudbright—suddenly Brynne realized where she had heard the familiar-sounding name before. At the turn of the century, the Kirkcudbright school of painting was known for its bold use of color. Brynne thought it was still an art colony, if vague memory was correct.

Then Brynne remembered something else. Two years earlier, Allen had given her a book about castles in Scotland. He was aware of her interest in that country, and had said teasingly, "Maybe your ancestral home is in here."

Now, where did I put that book? Brynne asked herself. She looked, first, in the bookcase next to the fireplace, but it wasn't there. Then she went into her bedroom, to her desk, which was piled high with books and papers. She finally found the one she was searching for on the very bottom of the pile, and carried it back into the living room.

Curling up on the sofa once more, she leafed through the pages. She came immediately to Allen's inscription, on the inside cover, written in his boyish scrawl—"To Brynne, I know your heart is in the Highlands. Enjoy your journey as you walk with Sir Walter Scott. You make my own journey through life a delightful adventure. Love, Allen."

For a moment Brynne's eyes misted with tears, but she fought them back and went on. It was a large coffee-table book, with full-page color photographs and brief descriptions of each castle, including amusing anecdotes about the ghosts that supposedly haunted most of them. She found Castle Fraser quickly. The description matched the one in the magazine. But it went on to say that the resident ghost was a young woman named Laurie Fraser, whose lover was killed at the Battle of Flodden in 1513. According to legend, Castle Fraser hadn't been an entirely happy place since that time.

Very romantic and appropriate, Brynne thought, amused, as she casually leafed through the rest of the pages. On the last page, she saw a photograph that she didn't remember noticing before. It was the author, Ross Fleming, and the photographer, Tam Stirling, standing in front of a castle. It was a casual candid photograph. They were relaxed, smiling. Ross Fleming stood a head taller than Tam Stirling, and there was something about his attitude that suggested arrogance. Fleming had brown hair that glinted with gold highlights, and eyes that were some pale color Brynne couldn't quite make out.

At the same time, Brynne noted Stirling's flaming red hair and freckled face. Yet, for some reason, her gaze kept returning to Fleming. The vitae below the photo described the author as also being the publisher in charge of Pegasus Publications. So, Brynne thought dryly, he was in a position to indulge a whim. For whatever reason, he had wanted to write a book about castles; and unlike most writers, he didn't have to worry about finding a publisher.

Suddenly, something deep within her clicked. Ross Fleming wasn't the only one who could indulge a whim. She sat absolutely rigid for a moment, thinking furiously. She *could* do it, she could buy the castle—if she sold the gallery. Without thinking further, she picked up the telephone on the end table next to the sofa and dialed a number.

"Hello?"

"Jason, it's Brynne."

"Brynne, love, it's good to hear from you. Is everything all right?"

"Jason, I've no time to chat right now. I just want to ask one thing. Are you still interested in buying the gallery?"

"Of course!" The voice on the other end of the line was both surprised and delighted. "Don't tell me you've finally decided to sell?"

"Yes, but only for the right price. Two hundred thousand, take it or leave it."

"You sound very determined. Was it anything I said this morning that made you change your mind?"

"In a roundabout way, yes. I just decided suddenly that I'd like to sell. But I may not feel this way in the morning, so if you're not interested . . ."

"No, no, Brynne, I didn't mean that. Two hundred thousand dollars, you say? Including the stock, I presume?"

"Yes, and all the furnishings."

"Even Allen's paintings?"

Brynne hesitated. Finally she answered firmly, "Yes."

"You've got a deal. I'll call my lawyer in the morning. On second thought, I'll call him at home tonight. I don't want to give you time to have second thoughts."

"Then it's a deal?"

"Exactly." He paused, then went on, "What are you going to do with yourself now?"

"You wouldn't believe me if I told you, Jason."

"Mm, sounds intriguing. I'll tell you what, why don't we celebrate this auspicious occasion? I could be over in ten minutes with a bottle of Moët et Chandon and my Ravel records."

"This is strictly business. I'll see you when you've got two hundred thousand dollars for me."

"Brynne, love, you're a hardhearted woman."

"*You* taught me, Jason. You said there's a time to smile and lower the price, and a time to smile and stand firm."

"What are you doing now?"

"I'm smiling."

"And?"

"And standing firm."

"You are impossible."

"And *you* are incorrigible."

"I try."

"Good-bye, Jason."

Brynne hung up with a strong feeling of having burned her bridges behind her. There could be no going back now. In one fell swoop she had cut her ties to Carmel and to Allen's memory. She didn't know exactly what would happen in Scotland. But somehow she suspected it would be a romantic adventure.

Chapter Two

*Y*ou did *what?*" Jane McAllister asked her sister in amazement.

"I sold the gallery. And I'm thinking of buying a castle in Scotland."

Jane and Brynne were sitting in a charming little bakery-restaurant called La Patisserie. It was decorated in a country-French motif with a blue-tiled fireplace adding warmth to the small dining room. They had eaten a delicious quiche lorraine for lunch and were now lingering over coffee and chocolate éclairs.

"Here," Brynne said, "is the photo the real-estate agent sent. It's the one they used in the magazine advertisement where I first saw it."

Jane gazed at the photo skeptically. She was of medium height, like Brynne, but there the resemblance stopped. While Brynne was fair, Jane was dark, with chocolate-brown eyes and dark-chestnut hair. She wore her hair straight and long, nearly to her waist, pulling it back from her oval face with tortoiseshell combs.

Everything about her was simple and natural, from her complete absence of makeup to her worn jeans. But, almost in spite of herself, she was extremely pretty. That, and her intriguing the-world-be-damned attitude, fascinated men. From the time she was fourteen, she'd never had a shortage of admirers.

Jane was outspoken, opinionated, and not overly sensitive to the feelings of the young men who flocked around her. Once, when she showed a complete lack of concern for a young man who was obviously crazy about her, Brynne told her, "You'll meet your match someday. Someone who will give you a taste of your own medicine."

"No way," Jane replied emphatically. "I'll never let anyone else have the upper hand."

And she didn't.

Now, as Jane handed the photo of the castle back to Brynne, she said, "It's a castle, all right. But *why* would you want to buy it?"

Brynne hesitated. She wasn't at all sure she could explain her feelings to her sister. She couldn't entirely explain them to herself. "I told you recently that I wanted a change in my life," she finally said.

"A *change* I can understand—a weekend in Acapulco, a new wardrobe, even a drastic haircut. But a *castle* . . ."

Brynne said quickly, "Janey, come with me. Just for a visit. I'm going to look the place over before committing myself."

Jane was thoughtful for a moment. "Perhaps it *would* be good for me to get away for a while."

"Come on," Brynne urged persuasively. "We'll have an adventure, get out of the old dull routine. Besides, it will be fun to see where our ancestors came from."

"If they had enough sense to leave the place, why should we go back?"

Brynne smiled indulgently. "You're just being stubborn."

"And you're being crazy. Brynne, this isn't like you."

"That's just the point. I'm tired of doing what everyone else expects me to do. Just *once* I want to do something crazy, something impulsive. Something for *me*. Without being concerned about anyone else."

Jane paused, eyeing Brynne thoughtfully. Then she shrugged her shoulders and said breezily, "You're right. It's *your* life and it's about time you did what you please with it. After all, I took my share of our inheritance and plunged it into a catering business that still doesn't make much of a profit."

"Thanks for understanding, Janey."

"And I'll be crazy, too," Jane went on, getting into the mood of wild abandon. "I'll come with you to see this godforsaken place. Who knows—maybe once you see it, you'll turn around and come straight back to Carmel."

Brynne hugged Jane tightly. "You're wrong, you know. I'm going to love it. I just know it.

But thanks for going with me. I'm a little bit nervous about kicking over the traces for the first time."

"I should think so. Where the hell is this moldy old ruin, anyway?"

"It isn't a moldy old ruin. It's basically in good shape, according to the realtor. It just needs some paint and a little plumbing work. And it's a cozy place—only about three thousand square feet. So it's not some massive palace you could get lost in."

"Well, where is this 'cozy' castle, then?"

"In Kirkcudbright, a village on the southwestern coast of Scotland. It's in the border country. You know, where Sir Walter Scott set his romances."

"Hey!" Jane exclaimed, her expression brightening. "Maybe this place comes equipped with a romantic knight in shining armor! How would you like to be carried off into the heather?"

"The only romance I'm looking for is the romantic atmosphere of old stone, moats and drawbridges. For six years my life was dominated by Allen. I loved him and I was happy with him. But now I want to be my own person, living alone and liking it, thank you."

"What are you going to do, wall yourself up in an ivory tower?"

"I'm going to renovate that castle and live in it. And I'm going to paint again," Brynne insisted stubbornly.

"When did you want to leave?"

"The end of the month. Can you arrange things by then?"

"Yes. There's nothing on my schedule after the eighteenth."

"Jason's taking over the gallery on the fifteenth. I'm going to pack up my personal belongings, except for the clothes I'll take with me, and put them in storage. Even if I don't buy the castle, I think I'll stay over there for a while and travel."

"What about the house?"

"I've found a house-sitter, a college student, to stay for a while. If I do decide to buy the castle, I'll put the house up for sale."

"Well, I'm glad you're not getting rid of it yet. I just can't believe that you'll end up staying over there. Now, getting back to this knight in shining armor . . ."

"Forget it, Jane."

"Okay. It was just a thought. By the way, what will you tell all your friends here? Or were you planning on sneaking off in the middle of the night?"

Brynne laughed. "I've already told everyone that I'm taking an extended vacation after selling the gallery."

"Well, I'd better get back to Monterey and start making my own arrangements," Jane said, picking up her purse and getting to her feet. "I've got to find someone to water my plants and feed the cat. See you later."

"'Bye."

When she was gone, Brynne looked again at the photo of the castle.

It *is* the sort of place where you might expect to run into a dashing knight, she admitted to herself.

At thirteen, when she was immersed in

Scott's novels, she had found the idea of chivalric love wonderful. She vividly daydreamed about how it must have been when knights fought to the death for their lady loves, when chivalry ruled the relationships between men and women, and the rule of the Round Table was to "love one only and to cleave to her."

Now Brynne knew a great deal more about love and had lost her illusions about it. Though her love for Allen was, on the whole, happy, there was another side to it. Loving a man, making a commitment to him, meant giving up a great deal of freedom. It sometimes meant losing your own identity in someone else's.

No, Brynne thought, I don't want a knight in shining armor now. I want adventure and fun. I want to be blissfully selfish for a while, to think of no one but myself. I want to find a place where I can finally find out who I am.

She hoped Castle Fraser would be that place.

Brynne and Jane arrived at Glasgow Airport on the morning of April 28. They rented a car and drove down through the lowlands to the border country. Brynne immediately fell in love with the dramatic scenery of Scotland. She felt exuberant, her blood raced, and her pale complexion brightened.

There was something mesmerizing about the glens, the white torrents of rivers, the way the mountains lay in purple layers against the sky, and the little white homes in the hollows of the hills. The atmosphere was redolent of clans and bagpipes, twirling kilts and tam-o'-shanters, Shetland ponies and Scotch whiskey.

As they got to the border country, they saw castles in ruins and Gothic skeletons of abbeys dotting the ballad-rich land of plunder and destruction. Here were fought the endless battles between England and Scotland when the Scots were still fiercely independent.

Finally, early in the afternoon, they arrived at Kirkcudbright. The seaside village was one of the most picturesque towns in Scotland. A quay jutted out into the sea, and the wide streets were fronted by gay, multicolored houses. It was a cold but sunny day, the sky full of rolling white cloud banks, and the hills and sea deluged with floods of radiant color.

The eighteenth-century lanes and narrow streets of the village were marvelously quaint. Signs over the shops indicated this was a lively center of weavers, potters and painters.

"Let's try that place," Jane said, pointing to a hotel in a Georgian-style building just down Old High Street.

When they walked into it a moment later, the hotel turned out to be fairly small and its appointments simple, yet it was colorful and charming.

"This place looks positively boring," Jane whispered as they walked in.

" 'Restful' or 'tranquil' would be a more polite way of phrasing it," Brynne responded dryly. "I like it."

"You would."

A plump middle-aged woman stood behind the front desk.

"May I help ye?" she asked amiably in a broad Scots accent.

"We'd like two rooms, if you have them," Brynne replied.

"That we do. How long will ye be stayin'?"

"I'm not sure. You see, I'm here to look at Castle Fraser. I may be buying it."

"Ach, ye'll be Miss McAllister," the woman said matter-of-factly. "Imagine that. 'Tis an honor an' a privilege, miss. I'm Sheila Lindsay."

"How did you know my name?" Brynne asked curiously.

"Donald Drummond told me a fortnight ago that the castle might have a new owner, an' if so he'd be renovatin' it. He mentioned yer name. He'll be surprised ye've come sae soon. But then, you Americans dunna' let the grass grow under yer feet, I ken."

Drummond was the man the British real-estate agent had recommended to handle the renovation if Brynne decided to buy the castle. He was a local contractor with an excellent reputation, so Brynne understood. She marveled at the fast way news traveled here.

Jane threw her a quick look, as if to say that obviously Brynne was bound to be a hot topic of local conversation.

"I'm glad you know Mr. Drummond," Brynne responded politely, ignoring Jane. "Can you tell me where his office is?"

"Ye're wantin' tae see the castle, I reckon. Fortunately, Donald's in town today. Most times, ye'll never ken where to find him. He travels over all o' Galloway an' Dumphries on one job or another. Just go down the High Street that way," she said, pointing out the window, "an' walk for two blocks till ye come to a close wi' a bright blue gate. His office is in there."

"Thank you."

"If ye'll leave yer car keys, I'll ha' the boy park it in the garage and bring yer bags in while ye see Donald."

Brynne handed her the keys, thanking her again.

A few minutes later, she and Jane reached the blue gate. The close was a cobbled courtyard with doors opening off it. Picking their way through a profusion of bicycles, they found a door with the sign "Donald Drummond, Master Mason."

Inside, Brynne found a heavyset, graybearded, elderly man. Immense and muscular, he had rolled up his white shirt sleeves above his elbows, revealing brawny forearms. When she introduced herself and Jane, the man responded happily, "Nice to meet ye," pumping Brynne's hand enthusiastically. "I didna' expect ye sae soon."

"Actually, I'm rather anxious to see Castle Fraser," Brynne replied pointedly.

"The agent did say ye'd never set eyes on the place. I must admit it's a bit tumbledown now. But the structure is sound an' it willna' take long to set it to rights. Ye willna' be disappointed, miss, that I promise."

"I'm sure I won't be. Could we possibly see it this afternoon?"

"You mean right now?" Donald asked, surprised.

"If you don't mind. Naturally, I'm curious about it."

"Naturally. Well, let's go, then. My car's parked on the street."

"Is it far to the castle?" Jane asked, clearly wondering how long it would take to get this over with.

"No, only about fifteen or twenty minutes. 'Tisn't that far, really, but the road's no' so good."

As they drove through the lovely, gently rolling countryside, dotted with buildings made of the local red sandstone, Donald talked almost nonstop. He told Brynne that the local people were relieved that a person of Scots descent might be taking over the castle, "instead o' some Arab, like has bought half o' London, so they say."

Jane gave Brynne a surreptitious wink, and Brynne had to try very hard to keep a straight face. Donald was a character, almost too Scottish to be true. Yet she liked his open, friendly manner. And she appreciated the fact that he was reassuring her she was welcome in Kirkcudbright. She had been worried that she would be viewed as an outsider, an interloper. But apparently her name took care of that, even though her family hadn't set foot in Scotland for almost a hundred years.

Once a Scot, always a Scot, Brynne thought, amused. Yet she felt it was true, in a sense. She had loved Scotland from the moment she first saw it. She had even felt, in a strange way, as if she were coming home.

Fanciful as it sounded, this country stirred her blood.

"You know, Sir Walter Scott set his novel *Redgauntlet* here," Brynne commented.

"Aye, this area has a fierce history. 'Tis only a small corner o' Scotland, but it faces Solway firth with the English shore on the other side. It was hotly contested for centuries because it lay athwart the main route to the north through the hills. It knew not merely raiders, but great armies, including the Romans," Donald finished impressively.

Suddenly he gestured ahead and said proudly, "Ah, there's the castle."

Anxiously Brynne peered ahead at the thing Jane had already dubbed "Brynne's folly."

"It looks more like a fortified house than a castle," Jane commented critically.

"Aye, 'tis a bit like a fortress out o' medieval France," Donald replied as they stopped in front of the castle.

Brynne got out of the car and walked up to the castle. Great double towers dominated the entrance, and there were towers at the other angles of its triangular plan. Turrets and parapet walks were corbeled out, enriching the walls with shadowed cornices. The interior court was overlooked by great windows surmounted by ornate carving, clearly put in at a later date.

Donald pointed out the grooves for the portcullis and drawbridge machinery, and close by a small hole through which molten lead or quicklime could be poured on men assaulting the entrance defenses.

"Well, it certainly is *old*," Jane commented, unimpressed.

But Brynne was paying no attention.

The wall that surrounded the courtyard was crumbling badly, but the two wings of the house itself were in perfect condition. Brynne had been afraid that she would be disappointed; that when she saw it, she would ask herself why on earth she had done such a silly, impulsive thing as to sell the gallery with the idea of buying this place.

But now, as she looked at it with a rapt expression on her lovely face, her doubts disappeared. The castle was everything she had hoped it would be.

"Let me show you the interior," Donald said as he walked up to stand beside her. "I have a key."

He unlocked the large double oak doors, and Brynne stepped across the stone threshold into her castle. The entryway was two stories tall. In the middle, a spacious oak staircase led up to a landing overlooking the hall. To the left of the hall was a large dining room, and beyond it an antiquated kitchen.

To the right was the drawing room. Donald explained that it had once been the banquet hall before the castle was renovated. Despite the dust of years, it was a beautiful room, with French doors leading off onto a stone terrace at the rear of the castle. The huge stone fireplace, emblazoned with the Fraser coat of arms, indicated the tremendous age of the room.

"'Twas made to look like a Georgian salon,"

Donald went on, "but ye can still imagine what it must've been like when it was the baronial hall o' a powerful lord."

"What family did the castle belong to?" Brynne asked.

"Oh, several through the years. The Frasers, o' course, built it originally, but then it passed into other hands. As politics changed and allegiances shifted, it was given first to one family, then another, dependin' on whom the crown wanted to reward or punish."

As his deep voice droned on, recounting the history of the castle, Brynne found herself daydreaming, imagining this room as it must once have been . . . the fireplace giving off the distinctive scent of a huge peat fire, tapestries covering the walls, the stone floor strewn with rushes and sweet herbs, hounds waiting impatiently by the long trestle table for bones to be thrown to them. . . .

And standing there arrogantly, looking as if he owned the world and her as well, a tall man in a red-and-black kilt, his pale eyes hungry with desire for her. . . .

"Brynne!"

Jane's voice, and her hand on Brynne's arm, jolted Brynne out of her strange reverie.

"What?" Brynne finally managed to ask. Looking around at the room, she blinked confusedly. Suddenly it all seemed so different, so changed.

"I've been talking to you and you haven't heard a word I've said. Are you okay?"

"Of course."

"Well, you were a million miles away for a minute."

"I was just . . . lost in thought."

"I can imagine. You must be wondering what you've gotten yourself into."

"Jane! I'm thinking no such thing! I *love* this place. Don't you?"

"Well, I have to admit it's kind of quaint. But, Brynne, it's *filthy.*"

"It won't be for long." Turning to Donald, who was standing across the room, Brynne said, "I'm going to buy it. How long will it take you to renovate it?"

"Depends on what you want done. Cleaning it up an' paintin' willna' take long. But if you want a modern kitchen an' bathroom—"

"I do," Brynne interrupted firmly. "There are some modern conveniences I'd rather not do without. But I want the rest kept as it is. Just cleaned up and painted, as you suggested."

"Well, I can ha' the whole thing done in two months, then."

"One month, please," Brynne begged. "I'm anxious to move in."

Donald smiled broadly. "Ach, yer a lady after me own heart, Miss McAllister. I'll make Castle Fraser a showplace once more, just for you. An' inside a month ye'll be sleepin' under this roof."

"Under my *own* roof," Brynne corrected him. This was her home now. She felt it strongly. And she couldn't wait to move in.

They went through the rest of the castle then. The second floor had three large bedrooms, and the third floor had several tiny rooms that had obviously once been servants' quarters. Brynne asked Donald to knock down the walls in the small rooms to make one large studio where she could paint. The tall windows would provide ample light.

As they walked out of the castle several minutes later, Brynne stopped to look at it pensively. "You know, this place gives me a funny feeling, somehow. It has a sad atmosphere."

"'Tis true," Donald agreed emphatically. "The tears o' women work their way into the stone o' buildings. Castle Fraser is a sad place even now because o' the tragedy o' Laurie Fraser."

Brynne smiled indulgently. "So, you believe that legend?"

"'Tis no' a legend, miss, 'tis fact. Laurie Fraser fell in love wi' the Lord of the Isles himself, one o' the most powerful o' the Highland chieftains. But Laurie was proud an' high-spirited, determined not to be dominated by any man. Marriage then was like prison for a woman, ye see."

"I've heard the story," Brynne said gently, trying not to sound too critical. She didn't want to insult Donald, who clearly believed strongly in the tale he was telling. "Her lover died at Flodden."

"Aye, miss. He begged Laurie to run away wi' him, to take what brief time they had left together. He said he would wait for her by the castle that night. But by the time she made up her mind to go to him, he had already left. Soon afterward, he fought an' died at Flodden, where King James IV of Scotland led an army to the greatest military defeat in the history of our country. Ten thousand men, most o' the nobility, lay dead on Flodden Field. An' the king died, too."

"And Laurie Fraser died without ever marrying," Brynne finished for Donald. "Do you really believe in 'ghoulies an' ghaisties'?" she asked, doing a surprisingly good imitation of a Scots accent.

"Perhaps. Perhaps not," Donald replied evasively. "You know what it says in Hamlet —more things in heaven an' earth . . ." His voice trailed off suggestively. Then he asked impudently, "An' *you*, miss, do *you* believe?"

Brynne hesitated. She did sense an atmosphere of pervasive yearning, a deep longing, that filled the castle, the way the scent of roses will fill a room. Sensing Brynne's reluctance to answer him, Donald continued politely, "Have ye heard o' the second sight?"

"You mean the ability to see into the future?" Brynne asked, while Jane listened skeptically.

"It can also mean seein' into the past. It works both ways. Some very sensitive people have this ability. My old grandmother, for instance, was the seventh child o' a seventh child, an' she had the sight. She lived near Culloden Moor, where a great battle was fought between the English an' the Scots centuries ago. There were some nights, she used to tell me, when she could hear the wild high skirl o' the pipes, an' the sounds o' battle, the screams o' dyin' men an' horses."

For a moment there was an awkward silence as Brynne wondered how on earth to respond to Donald's superstitions.

Then Jane said matter-of-factly, "We'd better be getting back. It's growing dark."

As they drove off, Donald said defensively, "If ye no' believe the tale o' Laurie Fraser, think o' this—a descendant o' the Lord of the Isles lives near here, in Fleming House, a beautiful old Georgian manor. When the man who was Laurie's lover died, his brother inherited the title an' married the girl who was the heiress at the manor at the time. Which reminds me, there'll be a big Beltane celebration there Saturday. Everyone in these parts goes. 'Tis a tradition that goes back to when I was a wee lad. You an' your sister should go, Miss McAllister. Yer part o' the gentry now that ye'll be buyin' the castle."

"What is Beltane?" Brynne asked.

"In pagan times 'twas a ritual to frighten off evil spirits an' witches. Huge bonfires, called charm fires, were lit. Nowadays 'tis just an excuse to have a celebration. Bonfires are still lit, but no one believes they frighten off witches."

"Sounds like the Fourth of July," Jane responded, smiling.

"Perhaps. Seems to me I've heard o' that. As I was sayin', you two young ladies should go. 'Twould be a perfect way to meet yer neighbors."

"Frankly, I would feel awkward going to a party where I didn't know anyone, even the host," Brynne responded.

"Ye know me, an' I'll be there wi' my missus. I was just talkin' to Ross Fleming the other day, an' he said to extend an invitation to ye if ye arrived in time. Ye'll be the closest neighbors to each other, an' is only fittin' ye meet."

"Ross Fleming?" Brynne asked with a start. "Is he the publisher who did the book about castles in Scotland?"

"Aye, the same. A fine book it is, too. I have a copy, inscribed by Ross himsel'."

"Brynne, a party would be fun," Jane insisted, interrupting Brynne's thoughts about the man whose book had helped persuade her to come here.

Brynne realized that Jane saw this as a welcome opportunity to do something besides sightseeing and exploring old castles. While Brynne could happily sit for hours painting or reading, Jane had to be constantly active.

"Well, if you *really* think it's the polite thing to do," Brynne said hesitantly.

"O' course, miss. I can assure ye the gesture will be much appreciated. It shows ye want to be part o' things. By the way, 'tis a costume party. We all dress up in fancy rigs. I usually come as a pirate, wi' a patch over one eye."

"But we don't have costumes," Brynne pointed out pragmatically.

"'Tis no' a problem, miss. There's a shop on the High Street that sells old clothes. Ye could probably find somethin' suitable there."

"Brynne, you'll be able to throw something together. With all your theater experience, it'll be easy," Jane assured her.

"Are you an actress, then?" Donald asked, unable to keep a note of surprise from his voice.

"Not really," Brynne replied, laughing. "I just participated in a local theater group back home. Actually, I did more scenery painting than acting. I'm really a painter."

"Ye'll certainly fit in, then. Kirkcudbright's chock full o' painters," Donald replied.

"Well, anyway, we'll work up some costumes somehow," Jane insisted. "It'll be fun."

"Okay," Brynne gave in, completely helpless under the combined onslaught of both Donald and Jane.

That evening Brynne and Jane had a delicious dinner of poached salmon at a small restaurant overlooking the River Dee, then strolled back through Kirkcudbright, looking at the paintings in the windows of the numerous art galleries.

"Just like Carmel," Brynne commented.

"A bit colder," Jane replied, pulling her coat closer around her. Even in late April, Scotland was cold, especially at night.

"Brynne—you're not really going to stay, are you?" Jane asked, finally voicing the concern that Brynne knew had been on her mind since they looked at the castle earlier.

"Yes, I am. I feel at home here, in a strange way. I'm not sure I can explain it. For one thing, this place makes me want to paint again. Everywhere I look, there are fascinating scenes to paint."

"But this isn't home."

"Neither was Carmel, really. We only lived there a few years. Before that, we traveled constantly from one army base to another all over the world. That was just part of being an army brat."

"But everything is so strange here, so different. I mean, they serve the salad at the *end* of the meal, for God's sake."

Brynne laughed. "I don't think it will be *that* hard to get used to the local customs."

"Don't you feel out of place here?" Jane persisted.

"No. In California I did, though. I felt out of place and out of time."

"That's just because you were saddled with responsibility so early. It made you grow up fast and take life too seriously sometimes."

"Do you really think I'm too serious?" Brynne asked, genuinely concerned. She had always thought of herself as a basically happy person who enjoyed life. To think that she might appear to be an old sourpuss distinctly unnerved her.

"Sometimes I think you're a bit too serious," Jane responded carefully. "I'd just like to see you enjoy life more, have fun."

"Okay," Brynne replied, smiling. "I'll go to this silly costume party and have fun. Will that satisfy you?"

"Well, it's a start," Jane answered teasingly. "What I'd really like to see you do is to cut loose and have a passionate, tempestuous affair with one of these rugged Scotsmen."

Brynne laughed good-naturedly. "Why don't we take one thing at a time. This week I dress up and make a fool of myself; next week I have a tempestuous affair."

"Okay, I'll hold you to it."

Brynne was smiling as they walked into the hotel, but her thoughts were already far away from Jane and her talk of tempestuous affairs. She was remembering Castle Fraser and the strange daydream she'd had there. She was beginning to suspect that the yearning she had sensed there wasn't so much in the castle as in herself. But she didn't know what it was she yearned for.

Chapter Three

The evening of May 1 was cool and crisp, but clear. The full moon hung like a huge orange ball low in a star-studded sky. Brynne dressed in clothes she had found at the shop Donald suggested. It had turned out to be an interesting little boutique. Some of the clothes were old worn-out cast-offs from the thirties and forties, but others were new copies of period attire—high-necked white blouses with leg-o'-mutton sleeves and slinky twenties shifts. Brynne found a bright red peasant blouse with billowing poet sleeves. A red silk ribbon laced up the tight bodice. To go with it, she chose a full red-and-black-plaid skirt that was hitched up one side to reveal masses of white ruffled petticoats beneath.

Brynne felt like a peasant girl in the outfit. She envisioned herself wandering through the hills singing "By yon bonny banks" and gathering purple heather in her arms. Then she laughed out loud at the silly fantasy.

She pulled her red-gold hair back with a white ribbon. Scrutinizing herself in the mirror above the dresser, she decided she was happy with the effect.

Then she went next door to Jane's room and knocked softly. A low voice that didn't sound at all like Jane said, "Come in."

When Brynne entered, she found Jane lying in bed holding a handkerchief to her nose.

"Jane! You're not even dressed! What's wrong?"

"It's this damn cold," Jane answered thickly. She'd had the sniffles for the past two days, and it was obvious now that they had turned into a full-blown cold. Pausing to blow her nose loudly, she continued miserably, "I feel *awful*. I've been taking aspirin all afternoon, but they don't seem to be helping."

"Oh, dear, maybe you should see a doctor."

"He'd just tell me to do what I'm doing—take aspirin, drink liquids and stay in bed. It's this stupid Scottish weather. It just isn't normal to be this cold in the spring."

Brynne smiled in relief. If Jane felt well enough to be angry, then she wasn't too ill, after all.

"You're just not used to it yet. You'll feel better soon. In the meantime, I'll ask Mrs. Lindsay if we can have a nice hot pot of tea."

"No, you won't," Jane responded firmly. "You're going to that party."

"And leave you here alone when you're

sick? Not on your life," Brynne said adamantly. Jane hadn't seemed herself lately, and
Brynne was beginning to worry about her.

"Brynne, I really want you to go. There isn't
anything you can do for me here. I'm going to
curl up with a good book. And I honestly don't
feel like having company."

"I understand, but I still don't want to leave
you."

"And why not? I'm not a child, as you
always seem to forget. For once, *I'm* going to
tell *you* what to do. Go to this party and enjoy
yourself. Remember what Donald said—the
local citizens will appreciate it if you make an
effort to participate in their social affairs."

Brynne hesitated. It was true that she was
concerned about being accepted in Kirkcudbright. Still . . .

"Jane . . ."

"I insist. Go to the party, and for God's sake,
do a little flirting." Before Brynne could argue
with her, Jane finished, "If you want, you can
get that pot of tea for me first. But ask Mrs.
Lindsay to put a drop of brandy in it, if that
won't scandalize her strict Presbyterian
soul."

Brynne gave in. "All right. I'll do it. But I
won't stay out late, and I'll check on you as
soon as I get back."

"I'll probably be sound asleep, especially if
you can persuade Mrs. Lindsay to go along
with the brandy. So don't worry about me,
and *don't* hurry home."

A few minutes later, Brynne brought Jane
the pot of tea, which Mrs. Lindsay had gener-

ously laced with brandy. But as she left the hotel, she was uneasy, not at all sure she was doing the right thing.

Mrs. Lindsay had given Brynne directions to Fleming House, which wasn't far out of town. Brynne drove through Gatehouse, a small village just north of Kirkcudbright, and saw the blue Wigtownshire coast gleaming across the bay in the late-evening light. Then she passed the old border keep of Barholm, with its whitewashed farm buildings, boats riding at anchor, and a wide semicircular sweep of bay. Then came Creetown, and after that the open road, winding and dipping on its route inland. The headlights of her car picked out cottages with roses and asters clustered against white and yellow walls.

Then she turned off onto the small road that led to Fleming House. Tall blossoms and golden bracken lay by the roadside. Brynne passed through an old stone lodge, down a long avenue bordered by giant red rhododendrons, through a small wood of silver birch, and came out into the front lawn of Fleming House. The house stood in the middle of rich, wooded, rolling parkland. Its turreted Renaissance splendor in pinkish local sandstone stood out unexpectedly in the otherwise empty countryside. It was massive, three stories tall, and made Castle Fraser look like a cottage in comparison. All the tall windows which covered the front facade were brightly lit, and the curving drive was packed with cars.

Brynne left her car behind the last one in the drive, then walked up to the massive double doors. A butler opened them immediately when she rang the bell, and let her in without asking to see an invitation. Obviously, Brynne thought, Donald was right. As she walked into the crowded house, it looked as if half of Kirkcudbright were there.

Brynne recognized the young woman who owned the shop where she'd gotten her costume, and a clerk in one of the art galleries. Brynne was relieved to see that everyone was in costume.

A young maid, primly dressed in a white-and-black uniform, passed by and offered Brynne a glass of champagne. Sipping the bubbly liquid, Brynne looked around for Donald Drummond. It would be nice, she felt, to have someone to talk with in this crowd of strangers.

When her eye was caught by a black patch and a brightly colored bandanna, Brynne realized that she'd found Donald in his guise as a pirate. Making her way through the crowd, she finally reached him.

"Miss McAllister, what a pretty sight you are! I'm glad ye could come. I'd like ye to meet my wife, Margaret."

Margaret Drummond was the antithesis of her husband—she was tiny, slender, and dark, with an olive complexion and black hair. Yet there was an impudent sparkle in her brown eyes that indicated she was his match in spirit if not in size.

"Pleased to meet you, Miss McAllister. Like half of Kirkcudbright, I've been dyin' of curiosity about the new owner of Castle Fraser. It was very nice of you to come tonight. I'm sure a party filled with strangers isn't a lot of fun for a young woman."

Brynne liked Margaret Drummond's delightful frankness. She replied honestly, "I *do* feel a bit out of place. But I'm glad I came. All day long I've heard nothing but talk about the Beltane celebration at Fleming House. The chambermaid at the hotel was full of excitement about it."

"'Tis a big event in these parts," Margaret agreed, smiling. "We're all glad the Flemings keep it up even though they're not really here that much anymore. Since she was widowed, Lady Grace has spent most of her time in London, where she's from. And her son, Ross, works in Edinburgh."

"I'd like to meet them. Donald told me they're my closest neighbors."

"Lady Grace isn't here. But Ross is around somewhere. We were just talking with him a moment ago."

"Probably seeing to more drink, judging from the way the stuff's disappearing," Donald interjected.

"*You* should talk, Donald, an' you on yer third glass o' champagne," Margaret chided him playfully. "Actually, I think I saw him head toward the ballroom. There's a band and dancing there. Ye should be in there, Miss McAllister, wi' the other young folk."

"All right," Brynne agreed, smiling. "I'll go 'mix,' as they say. It was a pleasure meeting you, Mrs. Drummond."

The ballroom was a huge room with a wood marquetry floor and tall French doors that were open to reveal a stone terrace beyond. At one end, a band sat on a raised dais, playing a surprising combination of contemporary music and Scottish folk tunes. The dance floor was crowded with young people, while couples of all ages strolled in and out through the French doors.

Slowly Brynne made a circuit of the room, wending her way through the crowd and finally wandering out through the French doors. Beyond the stone terrace was a broad lawn sloping down to a small manmade lake. The long spring twilight had finally faded to darkness, and on the lawn several bonfires were beginning to glow brightly. Soon flames were shooting high into the black sky. It was a breathtaking sight. Now Brynne understood how pagan Scots might have believed this would ward off evil.

To Brynne, the atmosphere on this crystal-clear spring night was redolent of the past: through the gloom of the night, a knight might come riding in search of love. The Queen of Elfland might emerge silently out of the woods to claim a soul. Maidens might listen through the long night for the returning beat of hooves.

On the night of Beltane, anything was possible.

What about me? Brynne wondered wistfully. Is there any magic in this spellbound night for me?

A bit embarrassed at her romantic imaginings, Brynne turned away from the bonfires and walked back into the house. She was just passing through the French doors when the crowd brought her up short against a man who was coming out in the opposite direction. Looking up at him to apologize for blocking his way, she met the most beguiling eyes she'd ever seen. They were almost, but not quite, green, a fascinating, changeable mixture of gold and brown and emerald. Brynne felt she could look into them forever without quite seeing all there was to see.

In the next few moments, as they were pressed together, Brynne took in his other features. Taken separately, they were unremarkable—an aquiline nose, a rather firm mouth, a square chin. Yet together the result was immensely appealing. The longer Brynne gazed at him, the more attractive she decided he was. As she looked at him, she also had the distinct impression she'd seen him somewhere before.

Then it came to her—the photo in the book on castles. *This* was Ross Fleming.

The surging crowd pushed them even closer together. Laughing, his mouth turning up into an appealing crooked grin, he said, "We seem to be stuck. Hope you don't mind. I certainly don't."

His Scots accent was soft, cultured, not the broad dialect usually heard in Kirkcudbright.

Brynne was suddenly uncomfortably aware of his body pressed against hers in the narrow doorway. Her full breasts were straining against the lacing of the tight bodice, and she realized for the first time just how low-cut that bodice was. There was an impudent gleam in his hazel eyes as Fleming boldly surveyed her appearance. He looked for all the world like the lord of the manor appraising a kitchen maid whom he might like to take for his pleasure.

Before Brynne could reply to him, the crowd surged again, and suddenly she and Fleming were pushed inside the ballroom. She started to turn away, but he stopped her with a hand laid lightly on her bare arm.

"Here, now, don't run off, lass. How about a dance?"

Why not? Brynne thought. After all, she had come to meet him. She nodded agreement, and Fleming whirled her out onto the dance floor.

He was taller than Brynne, thought not by much. She guessed he was about five feet, ten inches tall, though his lean frame made him look taller. A lock of his golden-brown hair fell rakishly over one eye. Despite his slender build, something about him suggested strength. The hands that held Brynne were gentle but firm.

He had taken advantage of the host's prerogative to wear normal dress instead of a costume. He was dressed in a tuxedo, but the shirt was open at the throat, as if he'd grown tired of being so formal.

Brynne was just thinking she should introduce herself, when he said, "I haven't had the pleasure of meeting you before."

"No," Brynne replied, feeling somehow reluctant to reveal her identity.

"Ah, a mystery lady," he teased with irresistible charm.

He wasn't drunk, but he'd obviously had enough to drink to be especially friendly. As they moved slowly through the crowded dance floor, he held Brynne just a bit too tightly to be entirely polite.

Yet she didn't resist. She felt strangely at ease in his arms, as if he'd held her before and knew the curves of her body intimately.

"Now, don't tell me your name, let me guess. Ben Dalbeattie said he'd hired a new barmaid. And he said her hair was the prettiest red-gold, like a spring sunset. Surely that must be you."

"Perhaps," Brynne responded, perfectly imitating a Scottish accent now. She enjoyed teasing Fleming, whose manner of *droit du seigneur* piqued her pride.

They were near the French doors again, and to Brynne's surprise, Fleming led her outside onto the terrace. The bonfires were roaring now, and most of the guests were beginning to gather around them.

Brynne and Fleming stood in a darkened corner of the terrace, all alone. Though they were no longer dancing, he continued to hold her.

"How about a kiss, then, lass?" he asked impudently.

"Would ye be tryin' to take advantage of a puir lass?" Brynne asked impishly, giving him a sidelong look through thick, curling lashes.

"No, merely sealing our friendship," he replied with that delightful crooked grin.

"But we havena' been introduced, sir."

"Then tell me your name."

"No, I dunna think I shall," Brynne answered with an arrogant toss of her silky hair.

"Now, what did Ben say the girl's name

was . . ." Fleming said thoughtfully. "Ah, yes, Mary. That's it."

"Mary's no' my name," Brynne replied honestly, her eyes meeting his boldly.

"Determined to be a mystery, I see. Perhaps you're not even real. Are you a ghost, come on this mystical night to haunt my heart forever?"

"I might very well be."

"No, that's impossible," he said definitely. "'Tis not a ghost I've held in my arms, but a flesh-and-blood woman. And I'll prove it," he finished, pulling her toward him and kissing her deeply.

Brynne was totally unprepared for the kiss and for the onslaught of emotions it unleashed within her. Immediately she lost consciousness of everything but the feel of him. The sounds of laughter, talking, crackling fire and music all disappeared. The taste of his demanding lips on her softly pliant ones, the possessive pressure of his arms encircling her, filled her senses, making her feel almost drunk with desire.

When he finally released her, she was shaken. Their lighthearted game of flirtation had turned into something unexpectedly explosive.

Catching her breath with difficulty, Brynne said, "Yer a bold one, sir. Too bold for a simple lass like myself."

Turning away, she ran back inside the ballroom, pushing her way through the crowd. Behind her she heard Fleming call, "Wait!"

But she ran faster, and in a moment was out of the house, hurrying toward her car. As she drove off, she caught a glimpse of Fleming in her rearview mirror. He was standing in the drive, staring after her perplexedly.

When she got back to the hotel, Brynne looked in on Jane, who was fast asleep. Brynne was relieved that she wouldn't have to talk to her sister. Jane's suggestion that she do a little flirting had had surprising results. Ross Fleming kindled feelings in her that were startling. They transported her to a plateau of desire she'd never before experienced.

And he did even more. When she looked into his eyes, she felt a strong sensation of *déjà vu*, as if she'd gazed into those pale emerald eyes long ago and seen both pain and passion in them.

Chapter Four

In early June, when the weather had turned warm, Brynne and Jane moved into Castle Fraser. The downstairs was finished, complete with a modern kitchen and a guest bathroom. The sitting room was painted a soft seafoam green, with furniture in a flowered chintz pattern of the same color. The drapes were of matching fabric, and the walls were covered with paintings by local artists. On the second floor, two of the bedrooms and one bathroom were complete. As Brynne had asked, Donald had knocked out all the walls on the third floor to make one huge studio for her to work in.

A gardener recommended by Donald had transformed the overgrown, tangled exterior into a model of Scottish landscaping. Bright flowers were everywhere, the ivy that climbed the castle walls was trimmed neatly, and a well-manicured lawn surrounded the building. Castle Fraser was as comfortable and warmly inviting as Brynne had hoped it would be. Even Jane could find nothing to grumble about as they moved their things from the hotel.

"I think I'll have a small dinner party," Brynne said as she was hanging her clothes in her closet.

Jane was lying on the bed, watching her lazily.

"Who would you invite?"

"Oh, Donald and Margaret. Mrs. Lindsay. The Flemings. Since we'll be neighbors, I'd like to get to know them. And I owe them an invitation after going to their house on Beltane."

"Didn't you meet them then?"

"No. Mrs. Fleming wasn't there at all." Brynne said nothing of her encounter with the disturbingly attractive Ross Fleming.

Jane looked at her quizzically. "You never have told me how the party was. Every time I ask, you change the subject."

"Don't be ridiculous. It's just that there's nothing to tell. I didn't know anyone but Donald and Margaret, and I didn't stay long."

Brynne carefully avoided Jane's penetrating gaze by concentrating on hanging up her clothes.

"So what are your plans now that you're actually in the castle?" Jane asked, changing the subject.

"I'm going to start painting. Tomorrow. All

the sightseeing we've been doing for the past month has made me anxious to capture some things on canvas."

Turning to look directly at Jane, Brynne continued soberly, "You want to go back to Monterey, don't you?"

"Yes," Jane admitted slowly. Her voice was heavy and her eyes didn't quite meet Brynne's questioning look.

"Jane, what's wrong? Ever since we left California, I've had the feeling something's been bothering you. Instead of enjoying this trip, you look lost and unhappy most of the time." Suddenly Brynne had a thought. "Did you leave someone behind—a man?"

"Yes," Jane admitted reluctantly.

"Janey! Are you in love?"

"Hopelessly, desperately, disgustingly in love," Jane answered, still not quite meeting Brynne's look.

"But that's wonderful!"

"It's not so wonderful." Taking a deep breath, Jane plunged ahead nervously, "You see, he's married."

"Oh." Brynne's tone was intensely disappointed.

Jane caught the note of disapproval.

"It's not what you think, Brynne." Her dark eyes were pleading, her tone urgent. "I'm not breaking up a happy home or anything. Todd and his wife have been having problems for years. If it wasn't for the children, he would have left her long ago."

"There are children?"

"Three. She's the sort who likes to tie a man down with responsibility."

"Todd had nothing to say about having these children?" Brynne asked tersely.

"I *knew* you'd react this way," Jane said angrily. "You don't understand. That's why I haven't said anything about him."

"I *want* to understand. Don't get mad. How did it happen?"

"I catered a party at his office. He's a doctor and he just opened up a new office with several other doctors. We talked for a little while after the party. Then he called me later. Things just sort of . . . happened." She added helplessly, "I didn't plan it, Brynne. It's not what I would have chosen. But I *love* him. For the first time in my life, I know what it feels like to want someone more than anything else in the world."

"But, Jane . . ."

"I know. But he's married." She finished defensively, "Like I said, it's not a happy marriage."

"I'm not passing judgment, Janey. I don't have the right to do that. I won't try to tell you how to run your life. It's just that I don't want to see you get hurt."

"He *may* get a divorce."

"Don't count on it. It doesn't usually happen that way."

"This isn't the 1950s, Brynne. I'm not playing a role in *Back Street*. Can't you understand how I feel?"

"I'm trying to. It's just that I've never seen you as the 'other woman.'"

"That's just a label," Jane shot back.

"It's *reality*, Jane." Brynne's voice had grown intense with conviction. She had never expected this to happen and had no idea how to handle it. She didn't want to antagonize Jane, but she couldn't pretend she approved of her situation.

"I hoped I could talk to you about him. I haven't been able to tell anyone because . . . well, *because*, and I want so much to share this with someone."

"I know," Brynne said, her voice softer.

"Todd is terrific. You'd like him if you met him. He's intelligent and kind and so sexy I can hardly stand it."

Brynne was tempted to respond that Todd couldn't be *too* kind if he was hurting two women, his wife and his mistress. But she held her tongue.

"Jane." Brynne stopped and looked long and hard at her sister—her baby sister, the one she'd always tried to protect. She knew she couldn't protect her now. "I love you. Nothing that happens could ever change that. I want for you whatever you want for yourself."

"Thanks," Jane said gratefully. "I appreciate it."

"Have you talked to Todd since we've been over here?"

"No. Before we left, I told him it would be best if we didn't call or write. I thought maybe I'd get over him if I didn't have any contact with him."

"But you haven't," Brynne commented matter-of-factly.

"No." Jane's voice was small, poignant.

Brynne wanted to comfort her, but she knew that was impossible. This was something Jane would have to deal with on her own. No matter how much Brynne might want to, she couldn't lessen her sister's pain.

Brynne sat down on the bed next to Jane and gave her a quick hug. "How would you like to whip up something marvelous for my party? You haven't cooked in a month. You must be dying to get back to a stove."

Jane grinned, trying to summon up her old humor and spirit. "Okay. But none of this dull haggis or smoked salmon. I'm going to show these local yokels what *real* food is all about."

Brynne smiled with her, determined to lighten the somber mood. But she was worried about her sister. Jane was obviously deeply in love. And it was tearing her apart.

Brynne sent out invitations the next day for a dinner party to be held the following Saturday. Everyone accepted, including Ross Fleming. His note explained that his mother was away, but he would be happy to come.

On Saturday Jane spent the entire day in the kitchen, preparing an elaborate seven-course meal, from stuffed-mushroom appetizers to raspberry bombe for dessert.

That evening, Brynne dressed with special care. She took a hot, leisurely bath in the bathroom that opened off her bedroom. It was charmingly old-fashioned, with a deep claw-footed tub and polished oak cabinets. Lush green ferns hung from the ceiling, and the wallpaper was an intricate pattern of tiny yellow flowers. When Brynne stepped out of the tub, she dried herself on a large fluffy yellow towel. Then she powdered her body softly with dusting powder, and put tiny drops of her favorite perfume behind her ears, at the base of her throat and on her wrists.

She told herself that she was simply in a mood to dress up, after a month spent mainly in jeans. But Ross Fleming was very much on her mind as she chose a sexy white silk jersey dress. With full sleeves caught tight at the wrists, a plunging V neckline and a narrow, clinging skirt, the dress made the most of Brynne's curves. It had a gold-and-white braided belt that matched the thin gold sandals she wore. She finished by putting diamond studs in her ears, and around her throat a gold chain with an antique heart-shaped pendant that she'd found at a shop in Kirkcudbright.

Her makeup was simple—a dash of gloss to make her naturally pink lips glisten, some lavender shadow to accent her tawny eyes, and some mascara to darken her light brown lashes. She pulled her hair back in a loose twist secured by an ivory comb, leaving a few tendrils free to curl softly around her face.

Glancing at the clock, Brynne saw that it was getting late. Her guests would be arriving any moment. She hurried downstairs to the sitting room and uncorked a bottle of Chardonnay that Jane had put on a table. From the nearby kitchen came delicious smells and the sound of Jane humming while she worked.

Brynne was just putting the bottle of wine back in the ice bucket when Donald, his wife and Mrs. Lindsay all arrived together.

They were all wearing coats, for it was cool

at night, even in the summer. As Brynne took their coats, Jane came in carrying a plate of steaming mushrooms stuffed with cheese and spinach. Jane was wearing burgundy-colored satin hostess pajamas, chosen because they were cool and comfortable to work in.

"If Margaret doesna' mind me sayin', you two lasses look especially pretty tonight," Donald said, smiling.

"O' course I dunna' mind," Margaret chided him lightly. "At your age, Donald, you're all talk, anyway."

They were all laughing good-naturedly when another knock came at the door.

"That must be Ross," Donald said.

To her surprise, Brynne felt her stomach tighten with nervousness, and a flush come to her cheeks. Steady, she told herself. There's no reason to be excited.

But every nerve in her body was tingling with anticipation.

"I'll answer the door," Jane said. "Help yourselves to the mushrooms. They should be eaten hot."

Brynne began pouring wine for everyone, for she suddenly felt the need to be busy.

A moment later, Jane returned to the living room. "This is our neighbor Ross Fleming, Brynne," she announced.

Looking up, Brynne met the gaze of pale eyes that were not quite green. She felt her heart leap. Fighting back her nervousness, she responded politely, "How do you do, Mr. Fleming. It's so nice to meet you."

He looked as stunned as Brynne had expected. But he kept his composure remarkably well. "'Tis *my* pleasure, Miss McAllister. And please call me Ross."

He was looking at her intently, as if he couldn't quite believe his eyes.

"Would you like some wine?" Brynne asked calmly. After that first moment of recognition, she was no longer nervous. She had herself well in hand, and was enjoying Ross's consternation.

Finally he replied, "Yes, please."

She handed him a glass and he sipped the wine slowly, watching her thoughtfully.

Brynne noticed that he was dressed casually in a rust-colored turtleneck sweater and a tan blazer of some light fabric. The colors went well with his own muted coloring—his light brown hair streaked with blond, his pale eyes glinting gold and green, and his light complexion.

As Brynne watched Ross with unabashed curiosity, Donald said, "I'm surprised you didn't meet at the Beltane celebration at Fleming House."

"In that crowd, 'tis understandable," Margaret broke in.

Brynne's tone was serious but her eyes sparkled with a mischievous humor as she responded, "Yes, and I only stayed a few minutes." She continued to watch Ross as she went on, "Frankly, I was insulted by the behavior of one of the guests. Apparently he'd had too much to drink. He was *very* forward— even kissed me."

"Indeed!" Margaret replied, shocked. "'Tis the worst o' these young men today. No manners at all."

"No, indeed," Brynne agreed, barely able to suppress a smile as Ross choked nervously on a bite of mushroom.

Recovering himself, he said easily, "I'm sure, Miss McAllister, you put the scoundrel in his place."

"As a matter of fact, Mr. Fleming, I rather think I did," Brynne replied.

A slow smile spread across Ross's face and Brynne responded with a quick grin.

Having paid him back for his impudence at the party on Beltane, she was now willing to move on. "Let me show you what wonders Donald's performed on the castle," she said, carefully changing the subject.

She led them through the finished rooms, and everyone was suitably impressed.

"Since I grew up near here, I've been here several times over the years," Ross said. "But I've never seen the place look so wonderful." Turning to Donald, he said, "You did a terrific job." Then, to Brynne, he finished, "And you, Miss McAllister, have marvelous taste. You've made this place a cozy, comfortable home."

"Thank you, Ross," Brynne replied, finally lowering the barrier of formality with him. "And please call me Brynne."

"Very well . . . Brynne." His eyes were watching her as carefully as she had watched him earlier when she paid him back for that stolen kiss. She had enjoyed teasing him, and she liked the fact that he accepted her teasing rebuke with such good nature. Now, however, she began to feel uncomfortable under that piercing gaze.

"We'd better go in to dinner now," Brynne said, her voice betraying her nervousness. "Jane hates to serve a meal even a minute late."

"Of course," Jane replied brightly. "Wine needs to be aged, but *not* food."

Jane's dinner was a huge success. She had outdone herself, and everyone complimented her effusively. Brynne and Ross sat at opposite ends of the polished oak trestle table and said almost nothing to each other during the elaborate meal. Yet every time Brynne looked past the low bouquet of yellow roses in the center of the table, she found Ross watching her interestedly.

When dinner was finally over, Jane served coffee and brandy in the sitting room. Everyone was in a mellow, well-fed, happy mood, and the conversation went on well past midnight. Finally Margaret told Donald that it was time they let Brynne and Jane go to bed, and they rose to leave, along with Sheila Lindsay.

"Thank you so much, my dears, for a delicious meal," Margaret said to both Brynne and Jane.

"Aye," Donald agreed, patting his ample stomach, "'twas a meal I'll not soon forget."

Mrs. Lindsay added her thanks, and Brynne got their coats for them from the small closet near the front door. While everyone else departed, Ross waited behind. Jane went into the kitchen to begin cleaning up, leaving Ross and Brynne alone.

"I'm glad we finally had a chance to meet *officially*," he said to Brynne. "You know, everyone at the Beltane party said I was drunk or dreaming when I told them I met a vision of loveliness who disappeared as soon as I kissed her. I was beginning to think you were the Queen of Elfland, come to steal my soul, then disappear back into the netherworld."

Brynne retorted, "Serves you right. What made you think I could be treated so lightly?"

"Something in your look indicated you might not resist. And you didn't," he finished with disarming candor.

Brynne had the grace to blush guiltily. He was right, after all. She hadn't resisted one bit.

"Good night, Mr. Fleming," she said formally.

"Good night, Miss McAllister," he replied, flashing her that devastatingly appealing crooked grin as he went out the door.

Back in the kitchen, Jane smiled at Brynne knowingly. "Well, he's *not* riding a white steed, and he was in a well-cut blazer instead of armor, but other than that he had a distinctly 'knight-errant' look about him."

Brynne didn't pretend that she didn't know whom Jane was referring to.

"Forget it, cupid. I'm *not* looking for romance, and if I were, I'd choose someone other than Ross Fleming."

"For heaven's sake, why? He's *very* attractive. In fact, the longer you look at him, the more attractive he gets. He's got a kind of subtle sexiness that sneaks up on you."

"He's also arrogant, pushy and probably a confirmed philanderer."

"Well, I didn't say anything about *marrying* the guy. But hopping in the sack with him might be fun."

"I've got a *lot* of work to do, Jane. It took most of my money to get the castle renovated and furnished. I've got to start earning a living now."

"You know what they say about all work and no play," Jane replied, handing a wet dish to Brynne to dry. "What do you want to do—turn this place into a nunnery?"

As Brynne dried the plate, then put it in the cupboard, she answered over her shoulder, "A little celibacy never killed anyone."

"I'm not so sure. You know," Jane added teasingly, "if you remain celibate long enough, you become a virgin again."

"Jane!" Brynne laughed helplessly at her outrageous sister. She tossed a dish towel at her, then, rolling her eyes upward, said in a long-suffering tone, "Where did I go wrong with this child?"

"I don't know, but it's too late to correct any mistakes now. Getting back to Ross Fleming . . ."

"If you find him so attractive, *you* have an affair with him."

"Not a chance. He only had eyes for *you* all evening. Don't pretend you didn't notice."

"As I said, this is all beside the point. I'm going to spend my time painting. I don't have time for a dalliance with a Scotsman, no matter how attractive he is."

"Aha! I knew it. You *are* attracted to him. He's just your type, intelligent, quietly attractive, terrific sense of humor—"

"I'm going to bed, Jane," Brynne interrupted firmly as she dried the last of the dishes. "Good night."

"Pleasant dreams," Jane said meaningfully.

In her bedroom, Brynne sat on the edge of the bed for a moment. She loved the way this room had turned out. The polished hardwood floor was covered with plush area rugs in various shades of lavender and purple. The bed, an antique four-poster, was hung with lavender curtains and covered with a matching spread. The sheer flowing drapes at the tall windows were of the same fabric. Tall vases of flowers were everywhere—on the nightstand, on the small rolltop desk in the corner and on the broad vanity table.

The windows were open on this early-summer evening, and a cool breeze wafted in, bringing with it the scent of the woods outside.

From the first night she'd spent here, Brynne had felt comfortable. It was what she had hoped it would be—a haven, a refuge, a place where she could enjoy being alone after years of losing herself in Allen's overwhelming personality.

Allen . . . For the first time since coming to Scotland, Brynne thought about him at length. He was a genius, a truly talented painter, the sort who comes along only once in a very long while. He and Brynne were the same age when they met, just twenty-four. Brynne had only experienced mild crushes before she met Allen. From the first moment they met, when he brought some of his paintings into her gallery, he pursued her with irresistible charm and determination. He was so full of self-confidence that it never occurred to him he might not get what he wanted.

Brynne lay back on the bed, her arms stretched out languidly beside her. She sighed softly as she thought of Allen. . . .

If I met you now, would I fall in love with you? she asked herself pensively.

She was different now, she realized. Too aware of her own fierce ambition to shunt it aside for anyone else. As wonderful as he was, Allen had required that he always come first.

No, Brynne thought, it wouldn't be the same if I met you now. But you were my first love, and there will always be a place for you in my heart that no one else can touch.

Reaching up, she pulled a pillow down and cradled her head on it. She'd been too young when she met Allen and fell in love with him to realize what was missing from their relationship. Ross Fleming, however, made her all too aware of what could be between a man and a woman. His very look was a promise of deliciously erotic secrets to be shared. He made Brynne feel as she had never felt before; as if he knew somehow what she yearned for, and could give it.

Shaking her head irritably, trying to push Ross from her mind, Brynne rose and began undressing.

The white silk jersey gown fell from her shoulders, past her slim hips to the the floor. She stepped out of it, then removed the rest of her clothing. Taking a sleeveless green satin nightgown from a drawer, she put it on, then hung up the dress. In the bathroom she washed her face, removing the makeup she'd applied so carefully only hours earlier.

Back in the bedroom, Brynne pulled down the bedcovers, then turned out the lamp and slipped into bed. Though it was late and she was tired, she couldn't go to sleep immediately. Try as she might, she couldn't help thinking about Ross. In a very disturbing way, he reminded her that she was, after all, no more than a woman, with a woman's needs.

She remembered the way Ross moved . . . with an easy, unhurried grace, as if the world were his and he could take his time about enjoying it. There was something irresistibly seductive about that slow, provocative manner.

Outside the open windows, the trees rustled gently in the breeze, and a golden sliver of moon sent only the palest moonlight into the bedroom. As Brynne's eyelids grew heavy and her conscious mind was taken over by sleep, it was Ross Fleming's eyes she was thinking of—those not-quite-green eyes. . . .

Chapter Five

Brynne was sitting in the courtyard behind an easel the next morning. It was the first time in months that she'd tried to paint, and she was finding it very difficult.

At first it had gone well enough. She had blocked in the outline of the courtyard with a free and swift hand. She wanted to capture the morning sunshine on the castle walls, the gray stone cool in the golden light. Contrasting with the somber gray background were the berries of a rowan tree, hanging yellow and red.

But when she picked up her palette and began to paint, she couldn't seem to get quite the right effect. She wanted it to be rich, lovely, stern. But the rhythms of form, color and light were off. Growing more and more

frustrated, she finally set down her palette
and painting knife and gazed at the picture.

Normally she didn't work with a knife. But
something about Scotland made her want to
try new things. Her usual style, misty watercolors much like Allen's work, somehow
didn't fit in this bold, exciting landscape. She
was reaching deep inside for facets of herself
that she'd never explored before. It was both
frightening and exhilarating.

As she was looking at her work in progress
critically, she heard the sound of horses'
hooves. Turning, she saw Ross Fleming riding
up on a gray gelding. He dismounted and tied
the horse to a tree, then sauntered over to her.

"Good morning," he said brightly. He was
wearing a white open-necked shirt and black
riding breeches, along with knee-high black
riding boots. There was something about his
casual, offhand maleness that was disturbingly appealing. Brynne found herself growing unaccountably shy.

"Good morning," she finally replied, not
quite meeting his gaze.

"Am I interrupting?" he asked politely.

"At the moment, no. I was just trying to
decide where to go from here. I'm beginning
to think the trash bin might be a good place."

Ross smiled sympathetically. "You've got a
good start," he commented, looking at the
painting carefully.

"Do you know much about art?"

"My firm publishes art books, among other
things. I'm no painter myself, but I appreciate
good art when I see it." After a moment's

pause, he continued curiously, "Is that why you came here? To paint?"

Eyeing him frankly, Brynne replied, "You think I'm a typical crazy American, throwing away her money on a useless old castle, don't you?"

Ross laughed, a nice sound, devoid of harshness.

"Actually, yes. You've done wonders with the castle. I never would have thought it could look so marvelous. But the question is, why bother? The land is basically useless, it can't be farmed. And you don't appear to be a wealthy eccentric." He finished pointedly, "Why *did* you leave California?"

Brynne wasn't inclined to discuss her very private reasons for leaving Carmel and making a new home here. She answered curtly, "I wanted to, obviously."

After a moment's silence, Ross continued, "I was talking with Donald Drummond this morning. I wanted to know about you, and it's been my experience that Donald knows all there is to know in Kirkcudbright. He said you were widowed last year."

"Yes," Brynne admitted tersely, unwilling to offer any more information on the subject.

"I'm sorry," Ross said simply.

"It's all right. Now it seems like it was a very long time ago."

"Donald said your husband was a well-known artist," Ross persisted, clearly not taking the hint that Brynne didn't want to discuss her private life.

"Yes, he was quite good." Then she added

firmly, "If you don't mind, I've got to get back to work."

"Of course," Ross replied. "I understand."

And Brynne got the impression that he did, indeed, understand. He understood that it wasn't her work that prompted her to dismiss him. It was his effect on her.

"Do you ride?" Ross asked unexpectedly as he untied his horse.

"A little."

"Good. How would you like to go on a picnic this afternoon? I'll bring the food, and I'll show you a bit of the countryside that can't be seen by car."

"Sorry," Brynne replied quickly. "I have to work."

"What about tomorrow?" he persisted.

"Don't you have to get back to Edinburgh?"

"I'm taking a long weekend. I brought some manuscripts with me so I could work here. I'm not going back until Tuesday."

"I don't think—" Brynne began.

But Ross interrupted her. "There's nothing to be afraid of. I assure you, I'm actually quite a gentleman. Ask anyone in Kirkcudbright. They'll give me glowing testimonials. I don't go around seducing young women against their will."

"On Beltane you weren't *entirely* a gentleman," Brynne couldn't resist replying dryly.

"You weren't *entirely* a lady." His insinuating tone, and the bold look he gave her, made Brynne blush furiously. She felt a crimson flush suffusing her cheeks and wished fervently she could stop it.

Ross continued, "That was different, anyway. That night was . . . magical. I think I was bewitched. At any rate, that's my excuse. So, what do you say? Tomorrow at ten?"

Realizing that there was no way she could refuse him gracefully, Brynne gave in. "Very well. But it will have to be a short ride. I really do have to work."

"Good. I'll see you then. And don't worry about the horse. I have a docile mare who should do nicely."

As he mounted his horse, he finished, "By the way, that painting's quite good. But I suspect you can do even better. You're holding back too much. You must learn to let go, you know."

In a moment he was gone. Though Brynne tried to get back to work, she couldn't. Her mind was on Ross Fleming, not the painting of the courtyard.

What a persistent, insulting, thoroughly irritating man, she told herself angrily. But deep within her she knew it wasn't only anger he brought out in her.

Later, over lunch, Brynne casually mentioned to Jane that she was going riding with Ross the next morning.

"Aha!" Jane exclaimed.

"There's no 'aha,' about it. I tried to tell him I was busy but he didn't take the hint. I just couldn't get out of it."

"Whatever you say," Jane agreed breezily.

Brynne looked up at her irritably, but didn't know what to say. Finally she replied, "It's going to be a *short* ride."

"Sure."

"Jane!"

"What did I say? I was simply agreeing with you," Jane responded with mock innocence.

Frowning, Brynne went back outside to her easel. But she got very little work done the rest of the afternoon.

Ross arrived promptly at ten the next morning, riding the same gray gelding and leading a black mare. Behind him a small wicker picnic basket was strapped to his saddle.

Brynne was in jeans, boots, and a red-and-black-plaid shirt.

"I'm afraid I don't have formal riding clothes," she explained apologetically. She felt decidedly shabby as she took in Ross's jodhpurs and tall riding boots.

"Doesn't matter," he replied easily. "No one will see us where we're going. And besides, you look adorable," he added offhandedly.

As they cantered off, Brynne felt herself blushing once more.

I've got to stop this, she told herself firmly. It's ridiculous to let a casual compliment throw me.

They rode for over an hour. To Brynne's relief, Ross said almost nothing. He let her enjoy the beauty of the countryside in blissful silence. It was glorious scenery. Deep red rhododendrons grew in giant clumps, along with azaleas, orange-stemmed birch, and tiny blue flowers that carpeted the ground.

Finally they came to a slight rise. Beyond it, the sea glistened a clear, soft blue on this sunny, cloudless day.

"Let's stop here," Ross suggested, dismounting and tying his horse to a nearby tree. As he took the picnic basket from the saddle, Brynne dismounted also and tied her horse to the tree.

"Feeling sore, yet?" Ross asked as he spread a blanket on the ground under the shade of a tree.

"A bit," Brynne admitted, grinning ruefully and rubbing her derriere gently.

"'Tis always hardest at first," Ross said. "You'll soon get used to it."

And will I get used to your shattering effect on me? Brynne asked herself silently.

Ross opened the basket and took out a bottle of Chardonnay in a clay wine cooler. There followed some scones and a jar of lemon curd to spread on them, bread and aged cheddar cheese, and thick-sliced ham. It was simple Scottish fare, but delicious-looking.

"I hope this is all right," Ross said, arranging china plates, linen napkins and silverware.

Brynne smiled. "Do you always have such formal picnics? I'm used to paper plates and ants."

"It's all designed to impress you. Is it working?" Ross asked with that endearing grin.

"I'll let you know when I've tasted the food," Brynne answered teasingly.

The food was every bit as delicious as it looked. When Brynne felt she couldn't eat another bite, she leaned back against the trunk of the tree and idly sipped the dry, light wine.

Leaning on one arm, watching her interestedly, Ross said quietly, "You know, after the party on Beltane, I began to suspect you weren't real but were a ferlie."

"What's that?"

"Oh, any sort of wonderful or mysterious happening. When I was a little boy, my nanny would sometimes ask me if I'd seen a ferlie while I was out playing. She meant anything unusual. Actually, anything can be a ferlie— from an especially beautiful sunset to a ghost or fairy."

"Were you disappointed when you discovered I was merely mortal?" Brynne couldn't resist asking.

"No. I was anything but disappointed."

Unable to meet his direct gaze, Brynne looked away shyly.

"I've seen a ferlie," she said softly.

"Don't tell me 'tis true what they say about the ghost of Laurie Fraser walking the halls of the castle!"

"No." Brynne laughed. "I don't believe in ghosts. I was referring to the castle when I first saw it. To me, it was a thing of wonder." Then she asked, "Do *you* believe in the legend of Laurie Fraser?"

"I believe she was a silly woman who couldn't make up her mind. I don't blame her lover for not waiting. Served her right for keeping him dangling."

"You think that's all it was—sheer female indecisiveness?"

"Of course. If the legend's right, she loved him. Why not go with him, then?"

"Perhaps because she was an independent

woman, with control over her own life, and knew she would have to give that up if she married. In those days, once a woman married, she became simply another of her husband's possessions."

"If he loved her, as they say, she would have been a thing of value to him, not a possession," Ross said adamantly. Then he continued thoughtfully, "Obviously you're very independent."

"Now." Realizing how revealing that one word had been, Brynne quickly changed the subject. "Tell me about yourself, Ross."

"What would you like to know?"

"For one thing, why don't you have a thick Scots accent?"

He laughed lightly. "Because I was educated in England. My English mother was determined that I would speak the queen's English properly. Actually, when I spend more than a few days at Fleming House, my accent gets thicker and thicker."

"You never mention your father. Is he still alive?"

"No, he died some years ago, when I was in my teens. He was the hard-drinking, hard-living sort. Rode to hounds one day when he was dead drunk and broke his neck trying to clear a particularly high fence."

"He sounds very different from your proper English mother."

"Oh, yes. Like night and day. My mother's family wasn't quite as aristocratic as my father's. But they were a great deal more genteel. They met during World War II, when he was on leave from the Royal Air Force in London. It was one of those whirlwind wartime courtships."

"That's basically what happened to my parents. My father was in the army when he met my mother in San Francisco. They had only known each other a few days when they got married."

"Were they happy?" Ross asked curiously.

"*Very.* I know it's the sort of thing that often doesn't work out, but for them it did. They loved each other very much. She was never quite the same after he died."

"What about your own marriage?" Ross asked abruptly.

"What about it?" Brynne answered tersely.

"Was it happy?"

"That's a very personal question."

"It was meant to be."

"I thought we were talking about *you.*"

"I've never been married, so there's nothing to talk about. You didn't answer my question."

"My marriage was *very* happy," Brynne replied firmly, defying him to contradict her.

"Is that why you left California? The memories were too painful?" he asked gently.

"Something like that." Then she added, "You're very persistent and more than a bit audacious."

Ross smiled. "Two of the enduring characteristics of the Scot are audacity and perseverance. There's even a Scots word for it— *smeddum.*"

"Well, you've got a great deal of *smeddum,* Ross Fleming."

"So, tell me, what did you do in Carmel?" he continued easily, ignoring the barbed remark.

"I owned an art gallery. My mother died when I was nineteen and left it to me."

"Nineteen's awfully young to be in business for yourself. At nineteen I was carousing at Cambridge, pulling stupid pranks and generally making a fool of myself."

Brynne smiled at his self-deprecating humor. "Well, I wasn't terribly mature, myself. I had to grow up fast. I couldn't have done it if it hadn't been for Jason."

"Jason?"

The tone of Ross's voice, and the curious look on his face, made it obvious he thought Jason must be a romantic interest.

Brynne hastened to explain. "He was a friend of my mother's, and has been a good friend to Jane and me. He's the next best thing to a fairy godmother. I think we all have people in our lives who have more than a passing effect on us, who help to make us what we are. Jason isn't exactly a genie, but he does help to make things happen for me."

"How?"

"Well, the day after my mother's funeral I was sitting in the gallery, feeling sad and scared. I had decided to run the gallery myself, but I had absolutely no idea what to do. Jason came in and said, 'Take off those grubby jeans and get into something silk and expensive. You've got to *look* like a gallery owner before you can *act* like one.'"

Brynne laughed in affectionate remembrance, and Ross smiled with her.

"So he *was* a fairy godmother in a sense," Ross commented. "He turned you from a college student into a chic businesswoman."

"Exactly. Then he made it possible for me to buy Castle Fraser by buying the gallery. I would have sold it eventually anyway, but he gave me cash immediately."

"Obviously not a poor man."

Remembering Jason's million-dollar home overlooking Pebble Beach, his Ferrari, and his predilection for rare, expensive things, Brynne smiled. "No, Jason leads a very comfortable life."

"What did he think of your trading in an art gallery in Carmel for a castle in Scotland?"

Brynne smiled ruefully. "I think he felt it was a rather unexpected thing for me to do."

"What made you choose Castle Fraser?" Ross asked.

Brynne almost told him: Because you made it sound so wonderful in your book. But she stopped herself. For some perverse reason, she didn't want him to know that he had influenced her life.

Instead she said, "Because it was available. And Kirkcudbright appealed to me for the painting."

Ross watched her quietly for a long moment, then said, "I can see that when you decide to make a change in your life, you don't do it by half."

Brynne replied thoughtfully, "I spent the first thirty years of my life being someone's daughter, then someone's wife. Now I've only myself to think of. It seemed an appropriate time to do something just for me."

"So you bought a castle."

"Yes."

"Some people might consider that a terribly romantic thing to do."

"That wasn't how I looked at it," Brynne insisted. "I wanted to get back to my painting. For a lot of reasons I felt it would be better to go someplace different to do that. Kirkcudbright is a logical choice, considering the art colony here."

Though she tried to sound logical and matter-of-fact, she knew very well her motivation was much more complex. Seeing the advertisement for Castle Fraser, then reading about it in Ross's book, a book given to her by Allen . . . Her thoughts stopped for a moment. How strange, she realized, that Allen should have given her the book that ultimately sent her to this new life, to this picnic with Ross.

"I see," Ross said, interrupting her reverie. "You're really quite practical. There's none of your parents' romantic streak in you."

He was teasing her and she knew it.

"What about you?" she asked, determined to turn the tables on him. "Publishing is an impractical, romantic venture if ever there was one."

"Not anymore. You have to be a hard-nosed businessman to succeed. When I took over Pegasus Publications ten years ago, it was failing miserably. The company had a fine reputation for publishing quality books, but the owners knew nothing of advertising, promotion, distribution, computers, all the things that make it possible to show a profit. We still publish high-quality books, but we also show a tidy profit."

"And what about the book you wrote? A book on castles, especially one that dwells on the legends surrounding them, is certainly romantic," Brynne persisted, forgetting that she was giving away the fact she'd read his book.

She was surprised to see Ross look a little embarrassed. And he didn't come up with a quick retort to her jibe.

So, she thought, you're vulnerable in one way. You don't like having your fantasies analyzed any more than I do.

This vulnerability in him only made him more attractive. Brynne wondered why a man so charming, successful and attractive wasn't married.

"You're looking at me as if I were a new species of fish," Ross said wryly.

"Sorry. I didn't mean to stare."

"What was on your mind?"

Brynne decided to be frank. "I was just wondering why you never married. You appear to be entirely eligible."

Ross threw back his head and laughed. "Are you wondering if there's a skeleton in my closet—an unhappy first love or latent homosexuality?" he asked, clearly amused. "Well," he continued, "the truth is much more dull. I've simply never found the right woman, someone I knew without a doubt that I wanted to spend the rest of my life with."

"It doesn't have to be forever. There *is* divorce. A handy institution."

"Not for me," Ross said quietly, but with an

undertone of determination. "I'm not the sort to hedge my bets."

A slight breeze came up off the sea, ruffling Brynne's smooth, straight hair. A thin wisp of hair blew across her cheek. Reaching over, Ross gently pushed it back behind her ear. At that moment, he was only inches from her, his body leaning across hers as he looked deeply into her eyes.

"'Tis a good thing we're both so practical, Brynne McAllister. If we were a pair of romantics, we'd be carried away by this glorious day and enchanting view."

"Would we?" Brynne asked, her voice throaty and breathless.

"We would indeed. Perhaps 'tis better to be a little less practical at times."

His lips found hers as his arms went around her, pulling her toward him. Her hands were pressed against his smooth linen shirt and she could feel his heart beating fast beneath her fingertips. There wasn't the unexpected surge of passion of their first kiss. Instead, there was a slow, sweet oblivion that made the rest of the world fade away. In its place was a feeling so profound, so wonderful, that it seemed unreal. Brynne felt that she was in a dream that would last for eternity.

When Ross finally pulled away, obviously with great effort, his expression was shaken. Brynne sensed that whatever she had felt was shared by Ross.

He looked at her for a long moment, saying nothing. But his pale eyes were almost emerald green now with passion.

"We'd better be getting back," Brynne finally said, finding her voice at last. "I . . . I have a great deal to do."

"Is it too soon for you?" Ross asked gently.

She knew what he meant. But she didn't know how to respond. "I don't know," she finally whispered.

"You had the courage to begin a new life. Passion is part of life. Especially for a painter. Don't run away from it, Brynne."

Brynne rose and walked a few steps away from Ross. Pushing her hands into her jeans pockets and squaring her shoulders, she stared at the sea in the distance. She knew she couldn't lie to this man, couldn't make up excuses. He would see through them.

Finally, throwing all caution to the wind, she turned to face Ross. "You don't understand."

"What don't I understand?" Ross asked, rising and coming to stand beside her. "Surely you know as well as I do that there was something special between us from the first moment we kissed. We connected in a way I've never felt before. I know it's the same for you."

"We've only just met. We don't know each other . . ."

"Those are lame excuses, Brynne. What's between us isn't the sort of thing that needs careful tending in a protected hothouse atmosphere. It sprang full-grown from our first look. What is it that's *really* holding you back?"

She faced him, her amber eyes blazing. "All right, I'll tell you. All of my life I've done what other people wanted me to do, what *had* to be done. I've had responsibilities and I've met them. When my mother died, there was Jane to raise. Then Allen to support, not just financially but emotionally. There never seemed to be any time for *me*. Now I have all the time in the world to find out who I am and what I can do. It's frightening as hell, but, *God*, I want it! I want to be *free*. I don't want to be tied to anyone by feelings of love or need."

"That's saying it plain," Ross admitted, his lips drawn into a tight line and his eyes even darker now with anger.

"You frighten me, Ross. What I feel for you frightens me. I could get lost in you, and I won't have that again."

"You think you have to make a choice between freedom and intimacy?"

"Yes."

"I see." He said nothing more for a long while. Finally he turned away and began packing up the picnic things. Brynne watched him silently, feeling more torn inside than she'd ever felt in her life.

The ride back to the castle was utterly silent. Neither Ross nor Brynne spoke until she dismounted in the castle courtyard.

"Good-bye," she said softly but with unmistakable finality.

"Good-bye, Brynne," he responded tightly. Then he turned and rode off quickly, leading the mare behind him.

What have I done? Brynne asked herself forlornly. But she knew very well what she had done. She had sent him out of her life forever. And though she already felt a growing emptiness inside, she was convinced she had had no other choice.

Chapter Six

*E*arly Tuesday morning Brynne went into Kirkcudbright to do some shopping. In the small village, shopping was not the one-stop-at-the-supermarket affair that Brynne was used to in Carmel. First she went to the butcher shop for meat, then to the greengrocer's for vegetables, and finally to the bakery for bread and scones. She was walking down the street, her wicker shopping basket swinging on her arm, when suddenly she saw something that made her stop abruptly.

Parked at the service station was a white Porsche, and Ross was leaning casually against it. He was talking to the attendant putting gas in the car. As he glanced up, he saw Brynne. Even though he was about fifty yards away, Brynne could tell that he stiffened when he saw her.

This is ridiculous, she told herself angrily. There's nothing to be embarrassed about. We'll be running into each other occasionally in a small village like Kirkcudbright and I'd better learn to handle it.

She forced herself to look as natural as possible as she walked on. But she was painfully aware of Ross's eyes on her every step of the way. As she passed him, she smiled politely and said, "Good morning."

"Good morning, Miss McAllister," he replied formally. Then he turned away to pay the attendant, who had finished filling up the car.

In a moment Brynne had rounded a corner and was out of sight of Ross. But her heart continued to beat erratically as a rush of adrenaline flowed through her trembling body.

The week passed quietly. Whenever thoughts of Ross came unbidden into her mind, Brynne forced herself to think of something else. Their relationship was over before it had begun, she insisted to herself. All that mattered now was her work.

But when the weekend came, she couldn't help wondering if he had come down to Fleming House or stayed in Edinburgh. As she painted Saturday in the courtyard, she half-expected Ross to call her or to come by. She reminded herself that she had told him in no uncertain terms that she didn't want to be involved with him. And yet . . . every time she heard the telephone ring inside the castle, she paused in her painting, waiting for Jane to tell her it was Ross. Every time she heard a car coming on the road, she looked up to see if it was a familiar white Porsche.

But he didn't call. And he didn't come. Brynne went to bed late Saturday night feeling unaccountably disappointed.

The next morning, Brynne went to church in Kirkcudbright. Donald and Margaret had invited her, and she knew they would be hurt if she didn't accept. The Presbyterian church was an integral part of the community, and most people in the village attended it.

The service was just beginning when Brynne entered the small, ancient stone church. She sat down next to Donald and Margaret, who smiled silently in greeting. As the congregation rose and began singing a hymn, suddenly Brynne noticed a familiar figure a few rows in front of her. The broad shoulders, the back that tapered to slim hips, the golden-brown hair that barely touched the collar of his white shirt, were all distressingly familiar. As Brynne tried to sing along with the others, she felt her throat constrict, and the hands that held the black-covered hymnbook trembled slightly.

Of all the places where they might have met in a small village like Kirkcudbright, it hadn't occurred to Brynne that it would be the church. There was no running away now. She would have to look at him during the sermon. And when the service was over, she would have to face him. It would be both impolite and silly to rush off immediately.

The service seemed interminable. Brynne tried to concentrate on the sermon being delivered by the white-haired pastor with the gentle manner. But her thoughts were all of Ross.

Finally the service was over. As the parishioners filed out of the church, Brynne stayed near Donald and Margaret. They stopped just outside the door to speak briefly with the pastor. As Brynne stood quietly, listening to the conversation between Donald and the pastor, Ross came out.

He was clearly surprised to see her. He paused in the doorway, then moved on. When he came to Brynne, he said politely, "How do you do?"

"Fine, thank you," Brynne replied with equally studied politeness.

He greeted Donald and Margaret, and complimented the pastor on his sermon. Then he turned back to Brynne and said conversationally, "What did you think of our church?"

"It's lovely."

"Yes, it's a fine example of seventeenth-century architecture. Actually, there's been a church on this site since the fourteenth century. The graveyard dates from then."

"Oh, really?" Brynne responded.

"In fact, Laurie Fraser's buried there. Since you're interested in her legend, would you like to see it?"

"Yes," Brynne answered. She was nervous about being alone with Ross, but she was at the same time immensely curious about Laurie's grave. The thought that Laurie was actually buried here somehow made her more real than the shadowy figure her legend revealed.

Ross led Brynne to the graveyard next to the

church. On this sunny, warm June day, it wasn't a melancholy place. It was neat and carefully tended. Even the oldest gravestones had been kept in good repair.

"Here's Laurie's grave," Ross said, indicating an ornately carved, obviously ancient gravestone. "I ran across it when I was researching Castle Fraser for my book."

Brynne bent down to read the inscription. It was worn by time and weather, of course, but it was still legible. It read: "Laurie Catrine Fraser, 1490–1565, 'Life, not death, hath been my foe; now released, to my love I go.'"

The poignant words brought a tear to Brynne's eye. Laurie had lived for over fifty years after her lover died, and throughout that long, lonely time she had thought only of being with him once more.

"How sad," Brynne whispered.

"A graveyard is always a sad place," Ross replied matter-of-factly.

Brynne stood up and looked at Ross. Trying to keep her tone as impersonal as his, she said, "Yes, but Laurie's life was so tragic. Her love for the Lord of the Isles never died."

Ross smiled slightly. This wasn't the irresistible crooked grin that made Brynne's heart go soft. It was a vaguely cynical, dismissing smile.

"You're too susceptible to her legend," he said, but his voice was kind; there was no edge to it.

"You weren't entirely immune to its power yourself," Brynne reminded him. "You wrote about it at length in your book."

As he had done on their picnic, when she accused him of being a romantic at heart, he seemed embarrassed.

"Just because I wrote about it, that doesn't necessarily mean I find it believable or even romantic. By the time Laurie died, she was seventy-five. She was probably senile. I doubt that she even remembered what her lover looked like."

Brynne looked at Ross intently. She didn't believe that he meant what he was saying. He was simply trying to appear practical and unemotional. "You don't believe that sometimes a love can be so strong it lasts for eternity?" she asked softly.

"Eternity only lasts until we die. I don't believe that Castle Fraser is haunted by a sad love. Do you?"

"I don't know," Brynne admitted slowly. "Sometimes . . . sometimes I sense something that I can't explain, a feeling of longing . . ." She stopped, shaking her head confusedly. It was impossible to explain this to Ross, who didn't believe in haunted and haunting loves.

Deciding to change the subject, she asked, "Do you come to church often?"

"When I'm at Fleming House," he responded. "It's expected of my family, since we're by way of being the local aristocracy."

They talked more easily then, of the church, the people in the village, the weather— anything but what was really on both their minds.

I feel like I'm in a play, onstage, repeating words that someone else has written, that

have no meaning to me personally, Brynne
thought. We're both being so carefully polite
and impersonal, and all the while there are so
many crucial things left unsaid.

After a few minutes of small talk, Brynne
said, "I'd better be going. Thank you for showing me Laurie's grave."

"'Twas no bother," Ross replied. "I'll walk
you to your car."

When they got to her small rented English
Ford, he opened the door for her. As she slid
behind the wheel, she looked up at him standing only inches from her. They were so close
that she could smell his special scent, a min-
gling of after-shave, pipe tobacco, and perspi-
ration on this warm summer day. She caught
his changeable hazel eyes looking down at
her. For a brief moment his expression was
open, unguarded, vulnerable. Their longing
for each other was an almost tangible thing
between them.

Then the moment passed. Ross said good-
bye and closed the door for her.

After only the briefest hesitation, Brynne
started the car and drove off, leaving him
standing alone, looking after her.

Chapter Seven

℞oss arrived back in Edinburgh from Kirkcudbright just before noon on Monday. He was due to meet his friend Tam Stirling for lunch, so he went directly to the restaurant instead of stopping at his office first. The restaurant, the Abbotsford, was a literary gathering place on Rose Street, a narrow street lined with pubs and restaurants. Ross ate there often, not because of the rather self-consciously literary atmosphere but because it was convenient to his office.

As he entered the crowded restaurant, he looked across the large room and saw Tam waiting for him at a table in a corner.

When Ross reached the table and sat down, Tam said brightly, "I've ordered us each a pint. No sense in wasting time."

At that moment a waiter set down two pints

of dark warm beer on the table, then took their order.

As Ross slowly sipped the brew, Tam watched him curiously. "You usually look refreshed an' ready to take on the world when you've spent a few days in the country. This time you look dead tired."

"I stayed up late reading manuscripts," Ross said tersely, not meeting his friend's look.

"Mm," Tam replied speculatively. Then he continued, "Kate ran into Vivien Tait the other day. The poor girl's wondering why you haven't called her lately."

"Tell your lovely wife to tell Vivien to stop waiting by the phone. I'll not be calling."

"She's a damned attractive girl. What happened?"

"Nothing happened. I'm just not interested in her anymore."

"I should have known. That's usually what happens with you. Your problem, Ross, is that you have a low tolerance for boredom."

Ross didn't smile as Tam had expected. Finally Tam continued, "How long have we been friends?"

"Since we bloodied each other's noses at age ten," Ross answered, a trace of a smile on his lips now.

"Damn right. Bloody fine way for a friendship to begin, wasn't it? But we took each other's measure early and learned to respect one another. Maybe that's why we've been friends ever since."

"What are you getting at, Tam? It isn't like you to be sentimental over a bloody nose."

"What I'm getting at is that you look as if something is very wrong. And I wish to hell you'd tell me what it is, instead of playing this strong, silent role."

Ross laughed softly now, amused by Tam's jibe. "All right. I didn't mean to come across as a martyr." Reluctantly he explained, "You see, I met a girl . . ."

"I knew it. Only a girl or imminent bankruptcy could give you that sick, hangdog look. But there's nothing unusual about your meeting a girl. You've met a lot of girls. I've always suspected you of trying to beat Robert Burns's record of conquests."

"Hardly likely," Ross answered with a wry grin. "I can't see myself having 'bairned' two lasses before breakfast."

"So, what's different about this girl?" Tam asked shrewdly, downing his beer and motioning to the waiter for another.

"For one thing, she seems to be immune to my famous charm," Ross said dryly. "She told me in no uncertain terms to leave her alone."

Tam was surprised. His pleasant, freckled face showed a trace of consternation, and his light blue eyes widened. "That *is* different. What's wrong with the girl that she doesn't recognize a highly eligible bachelor when she sees one? Hasn't she heard the statistics on the ratio of men to women?"

"She isn't interested in marriage."

"Is there some competition, then?"

"Not unless you consider a ghost competition. She was married, but her husband died some time ago."

"Is she being faithful to his memory? Something sentimental like that?"

"Not really. She insists she doesn't want entanglements."

"A lady who doesn't want commitment. Sounds too good to be true," Tam teased. But once again, Ross wasn't smiling. "So, tell me about this highly unusual young woman," Tam finished, as he accepted the new mug of beer set before him by the waiter.

"She's American."

"Ah, an independent lot, so I've heard. Where did you meet her?"

"She bought Castle Fraser and had it renovated."

"Ross, this is straight out of a fairy tale. A damsel in an ivory tower. The handsome knight coming to her rescue."

"Only she doesn't want to be rescued," Ross responded succinctly.

"To hell with her, then. I hate to use a cliché in such a self-consciously literary atmosphere, but there *are* other fish in the sea. In fact, Kate wants you to meet her cousin. I know the girl, and I can verify that she's not only pretty but also intelligent."

"No, thanks."

"Drowning your sorrows with other female companionship might be the best solution."

"I tried that. Last night I called Allison Lowrie. She's staying at a beach cottage near Kirkcudbright."

"Ah, Allison of the lovely legs. What happened?"

"I talked to her for several minutes, then

finally realized I had no desire to see her. So I made up an excuse and hung up."

Remembering the awkward conversation now, Ross felt absolutely stupid. It was ridiculous to be so captivated by a woman he'd only just met. And yet Brynne *was* special—a woman who bought a castle, who insisted on her own turf, who believed in a love that had defied time. God! He might have missed her entirely if he hadn't written that book with Tam. It was the information in it about Castle Fraser that intrigued her so. That, he was sure of.

"Dammit!" Ross finished tensely. "I can't get Brynne off my mind."

"Brynne, eh? Lovely name. And with a face and figure to match, I'll wager. You *do* have it bad, Ross."

As the waiter brought plates of steaming lamb and vegetables and crusty bread, Tam continued seriously, "I'll stop pulling your leg, m'lad. Obviously this isn't a funny situation."

He continued thoughtfully, between bites of food, "But try to look at it objectively. It was bound to happen. I've seen it coming on for some time now."

"Have you now?" Ross asked, smiling at Tam's self-confident air.

"Of course. You're bored with the usual girls. Running around, playing the carefree bachelor isn't so much fun anymore. You're ready to settle down, and you happened to meet this girl now. It's just timing."

"No, it's more than that," Ross answered firmly. "'Tis true I no longer find it quite so

exciting to wake up with a stranger beside me.
But there's something about Brynne. We connected in a way that's never happened to me
before."

Though he would never admit it to anyone,
including Tam, he had been lonely most of his
life. From the time he was sent off to boarding
school at eight, to his years at Cambridge,
when he was considered one of the most popu-
lar students on campus, he had always felt
intrinsically alone. He hid it well, projecting
the image of a confident, happy young man.
And much of the time, he was happy. But at
the core, he felt terribly alone. Only with
Brynne had he felt that profound connection
with another human being that overcomes
loneliness.

What would it be like to make love to her, he
wondered, to be part of her, bonded with her?

"Is she pretty?" Tam asked.

"Yes, but not as pretty as many girls I've
known. It isn't her looks, although they appeal to me. When I'm with her, it just feels
right." As if it were meant to be, he added
silently to himself. Aloud he continued, "I'm
comfortable with her in a way that I've never
felt with anyone else."

"Perhaps it's just the challenge of the
chase," Tam replied, grinning. "We all want
what we can't have."

Ross didn't respond. He was silent for a
moment, and the background noises of the
restaurant, the clink of silverware, the mur-
mur of conversation seemed momentarily
louder. He knew definitely that Tam was
wrong. He thought: When I first saw her, I

had the strangest feeling I'd found what I've been looking for my whole life.

Aloud he finally asked, "Do you understand how I feel about her? Or do you think I'm daft?"

Tam laughed. "I think you're definitely daft. But I *do* understand. Kate said she fell for me immediately upon laying eyes on me, despite my mop of carrot-red hair. It was only a question of bringing me around to see matters in the same light."

Ross smiled. "Kate's too good for you, you know."

"I know. Fortunately, she doesn't seem to realize it. But, Ross, are you sure your ego isn't a bit put out? When you're used to women basically falling all over you, it can be intriguing when one resists."

"I admit her determinedly cool detachment is a stimulating challenge. But it's more than that. She has the kind of sense of humor I like, and she isn't afraid to put me in my place. I suppose what I'm trying to say is that she doesn't cater to me, and I respect her for that."

"So, what do you plan to do about this recalcitrant young woman?" Tam asked pointedly.

Ross thought for a moment. Finally he said slowly, "I think it's time to storm the castle."

Tam smiled broadly. "That's my lad!"

Chapter Eight

*B*rynne was alone at Castle Fraser. Jane had gone to Edinburgh to do some shopping, see some movies, and "catch up on civilization," as she succinctly put it. She had asked Brynne to come with her, but Brynne was working feverishly now and didn't want to stop. Each day she felt better and better about her painting. She still felt she had a long way to go before she would be satisfied with her work, but at least now she felt optimistic.

As she went to bed on this warm June evening, she was utterly exhausted. She'd painted from dawn to early evening, when it began to rain lightly. Then she spent two hours arranging some things in her studio. She was so tired that for dinner she merely warmed up some Scotch broth Jane had left for her.

Despite her physical exhaustion, her mind raced with plans and ideas. To calm herself, she reached over to the bedside table for a book to read. What she found was Ross's book on castles. As Brynne thumbed through it, she came to the photo of Ross, looking arrogant and utterly irresistible.

Ross Fleming was the last person she wanted to think about now. He'd been nagging at the back of her mind all week, since she'd seen him at church on Sunday. Now she slammed the book shut and put it back on the table. Turning off the light, she burrowed under the sheet and closed her eyes, determined to sleep.

Through the open windows came the night sounds: frogs croaking and splashing in the small stream that ran near the castle; an owl calling forlornly; the slight rustle of the breeze through the trees.

With these sounds came the scent of roses, especially fragrant after this evening's brief, warm rain.

The breeze blew clouds across the full moon, tossing shadows over the walls of the bedroom. Then, as Brynne finally slipped into unconsciousness, an image came, moving and fading through the silent room as the shadows moved and faded: eyes the color of the palest gold-hued emerald. . . .

The wind moved through the trees, stirring the branches. Creeping vines shifted and tapped lightly against the walls of the castle. Sudden gusts rustled the beeches noisily.

Laurie found a lucifer and lit the candle in her bedroom. The room was suffused with a soft golden light, showing gold velvet curtains at the tall windows, a rose-wreathed carpet, glittering sconces on the walls. Then she lit the sconces themselves, and the room was bright.

Impatiently she moved about the room, straightening an ornament, turning back the covers of the bed.

Surely, she thought, he should have come by now. He has never been this late before.

Her logical mind told her not to be silly, but she was raw with longing for him, and every moment seemed an eternity. She imagined him riding through the windy dark, her light-o'-love.

He *must* come, she thought desperately. Without him, the night would be barren and cold, an agony of loneliness. As she stood there, tall and slim and raven-haired, she willed him to come to her.

She looked out of the tall windows, straining her eyes to try to see through the darkness. There was still no sign of him, no sound or movement save the harsh wind rustling through the trees.

In the stillness of the quiet room, she remembered when she'd first met him. It was at a ball at the palace at Falklands. His pale eyes raked her boldly; then he pulled her into a dance without bothering to ask her permission.

Angrily she had told him, "I'm Lady Laurie Fraser of Castle Fraser, an' you'll treat me with the respect due my position!"

He simply laughed and responded confidently, "An' I'm Richard McDonald, Lord of the Isles. Before I'm through, I mean to be lord of your heart, my lady."

And he was.

Now she fidgeted like a nervous cat, unable to relax. Until she was in his arms, she was only half-alive.

Suddenly he was there. She heard his heavy step outside her door, the hand on the doorknob. He entered, a tall figure in a dark cloak over a frilled white shirt and heavy red-and-black kilt. The Lord of the Isles.

"My love!" she whispered.

He threw off his cloak and took her into his arms. One deep, long kiss, then his hands went to the buttons on her dress. It slipped to her knees. She stepped out of it, and he pulled impatiently at the laces at her breast. Outside, a nightingale broke the night's silence with a short, melancholy song.

Her breasts were bare, then her hips, then her long, slender legs. A moment later he threw off his own clothes and carried her to the waiting bed.

"What delayed ye, love?" she asked.

"The king kept me. But hush, now, we'll talk later. Here, my sweetest lass, come to me."

His touch was delicate and warm as his fingertips caressed her bare flesh.

"I want you so, Richard," she responded huskily. "I though ye'd never come."

His touch changed. It was demanding now, and grew in intensity.

"Did ye think I'd lost my way in the dark?"

he asked, smiling. "Dunna' ye ken I would always find my way to you, my love?"

"Even if I were lost in the middle of the blackest forest in the world?" she asked, teasing him.

"I'd find you," he answered, looking at her intently. "I'll *always* find you, wherever you are."

They made love then, in the light, as always. They wanted to see each other. It was only afterward that they extinguished the candles and the sconces and lay together in the darkness.

As he held her against him, he whispered in a barely audible voice, "I love ye, my sweetest lass."

Turning to look at him, Laurie asked, "When did ye realize that? When did ye decide that of all yer women, *I* was the one?"

Her tone was teasing, but underneath lay a need for reassurance. She was proud, and this was as close as she could come to asking him for anything.

He smiled down at her softly. "I knew that first night ye gave yerself to me. Afterward I didna' feel boredom, as usual, but gratitude. I was grateful for the precious gift ye gave me. An' later I felt love."

His hand slid gently over the curve of her breast as he pulled her closer to him. "Yer my heart an' soul, lass. I'll love ye through eternity."

"Oh, Richard." Her voice caught in her throat as her eyes saw the profound love in his expression. She had never seen him look so vulnerable, this powerful Highlander. At that moment she realized fully the power she had over him, and she felt not triumphant but humbled.

"I'm yours, love," she said simply. "Now an' forever."

His pale eyes glistened brightly with love as he looked intensely at her. "My sweetest lass. My heart's desire . . ."

He murmured the words of love as his lips kissed the base of her throat, the deep valley between her breasts, the soft white smoothness of her stomach.

Her fingers twined tightly in his shaggy dark hair, and she whispered, "Don't ever leave me. . . ."

Chapter Nine

$\mathcal{B}$rynne woke slowly, dragging herself reluctantly back into consciousness. Her body felt heavy and sluggish, as if she had slept much too long. Even as she struggled with wakefulness, she realized she'd been dreaming.

Or was it a dream? she wondered. It had seemed so real. In her dream, she had seen her bedroom as it must have looked four centuries earlier. And Laurie Fraser and her lover were there. . . .

Slowly Brynne rose and walked over to the open window. Outside, everything was as it had appeared yesterday. Her car sat in the driveway, the grass cut short and carefully trimmed, not tall and unkept as she remembered from her dream.

A word came to mind—"empathy," the

power of entering imaginatively into someone else's feelings or experience.

Did I do that? Brynne wondered.

Yet Laurie was dead. Could feelings be passed down through time? Donald Drummond had said, "The tears of women work their way into the stone of buildings." If the color of hair or the shape of hands can be passed down through the generations, could a feeling of love and longing also survive?

Shaking her head confusedly, Brynne went into the bathroom and splashed cold water on her face. Her thoughts seemed to tumble over one another haphazardly, making no sense. Finally, she said to herself, "Enough of this!"

She dressed in her work clothes, jeans and a loose shirt, pulled her fine hair into a loose ponytail, then went downstairs. After a quick breakfast of toast and tea, she paced her art equipment in the back of her car. She decided to paint in a new location today, far from the castle, where she suddenly felt strangely ill-at-ease.

Brynne drove for a long while, finally stopping at a cliff on the Carrick shore. In the distance lay the Isles of Fleet. Taking out her equipment, she perched on a lump of granite and began painting. The strong wind that was blowing this morning, and the menace of a storm, produced beautiful cloud effects over the fretful-looking sea.

She used big brushes and a broad, sweeping style. It suited the day and the type of effect she wanted to produce. A gust of wind came up off the sea, making the easel vibrate. Then clouds came together in one dark mass, and the waves were topped with whitecaps.

Brynne was well into the painting, oblivious of the threatening weather, when the storm broke. The moment it started to rain, she scrambled to secure her wet canvas in a carrier, putting in the canvas pins and pulling the straps tightly. After putting the brushes in a case and the palette in a box, she collected the tubes of paint she had laid on the edge of the easel. Laying the tubes in their box, she folded up and strapped the easel, then ran through the rain for the car.

As she drove off, shaking water from her hair, she felt intensely disappointed that she hadn't been able to finish the painting. It was going well, better than anything else she had done so far. She could do it in her studio, but that wouldn't be the same.

Then suddenly she said out loud, "Damn! I completely forgot!" Tonight she was supposed to go to a dinner party at Donald's house. It was the last thing in the world she wanted to do right now, with a half-finished painting to consider. But she knew she couldn't get out of it.

Well, I'll make an early night of it and get to work first thing in the morning, she assured herself. Donald and Margaret probably go to bed early. And I don't think anyone else will be there.

But she was wrong. As she drove up to Donald's house that evening through a driving rain, she saw a white Porsche sitting in the driveway of his pleasant cottage. She knew very well whom it belonged to. No one else in Kirkcudbright could afford a car such as that.

At the same moment Brynne was telling herself she didn't want to see Ross, she was wondering how she looked, wishing she'd chosen something else to wear. Her Wedgwood-blue silk dress was simple, almost austere. The only thing that saved it from being plain was the bright fuchsia silk belt that cinched the waist. It was certainly not the most becoming dress in her wardrobe.

Telling herself she was being ridiculous to even think about her attire, she pulled her gray mackintosh over her head and ran up to the front door. She was grateful for the wide overhang that protected her from the rain as she rang the doorbell.

A moment later, Margaret opened the door.

As Brynne started to greet her, she looked past her into the house. Standing in the hallway, watching her with an amused grin, was Ross.

"Come in, lass," Margaret said cheerfully. "'Tis an awfu' night out. I always hate summer storms, they seem so unfair somehow. In the winter, one expects them, but summer should be clear and pretty. Let me take your wet coat. My, it *did* get soaked, didn't it?"

But as Margaret prattled on in her friendly, concerned fashion, Brynne was barely listening. She was looking at Ross and his pleased expression. She was convinced that he had somehow learned she was going to be here tonight, and that was why he'd come. After all, when Donald invited her to dinner, he said nothing of Ross.

As Margaret led her into the sitting room, a small, comfortably furnished room where a cheery fire burned in the huge old stone fireplace, Ross handed her a cup of steaming mulled wine.

"This will warm you up," he said pleasantly.

"Thank you," Brynne murmured, gratefully sipping the hot, spiced liquid. "I thought you were in Edinburgh," she said politely.

The mischievous twinkle in his eyes as he watched her revealed that he knew exactly what she was getting at. "I found myself missing the country. Thought I'd come back for a while."

"How long will you be staying?"

"That depends," he answered noncommittally.

"I was fair amazed when I ran into Ross on the High Street today," Donald interjected. "'Tis rare to find him down here two weekends running. I insisted he join us for dinner tonight."

As Donald rose to get more mulled wine, Ross said to Brynne, "And how have you been since I saw you last?"

"Fine, thank you," Brynne replied coolly.

"Been painting much?"

"Yes."

"Good. If you don't paint or fish, you can grow bored here, for there's very little else to do."

"I *never* grow bored," Brynne insisted

pointedly. "I enjoy the peace and quiet and solitude here."

"But surely it gets a bit lonely living out there at Castle Fraser, with no one else for miles around?"

"But I'm not alone. Jane's there," Brynne reminded him.

"Aye, but she's in Edinburgh now," Donald broke in.

Brynne could have cursed him for revealing that fact to Ross. Looking at Ross, she saw a speculative expression on his face.

"So, she's in Edinburgh. Why didn't you go too, Brynne?"

"I'm far too busy," Brynne answered tersely.

"But you should see the city. It's quite beautiful, you know. 'The Athens of the North,' some people call it. You'll have to go there sometime."

"I will . . . sometime," Brynne agreed.

Though Margaret was an excellent cook and had prepared a lavish meal, Brynne barely tasted the food when they went in to dinner. She felt Ross watching her. As the evening wore on, she grew more and more keyed up with an excitement and anticipation that she didn't entirely understand.

Finally, at eleven o'clock, she bid Donald and Margaret good night.

"'Tis worse than ever out there," Donald commented worriedly, looking out the window at the pounding rain.

Following his gaze, Brynne saw that it was coming down in heavy sheets now, thick and slanting, obscuring everything beyond a distance of only a few feet. The wind lashed furiously at the trees and the house.

"I dunna' like to think o' you drivin' home alone in this storm on that narrow, poorly paved road," Margaret said with real concern in her voice. "An' you no' used to the road yet."

"I'll be all right," Brynne insisted, but her attempt at confidence rang false even to her own ears.

"You can't go home alone in this storm," Ross said flatly. "What if your car broke down or you skidded on the slippery pavement? I'll take you. It's not far from Fleming House."

"But my car . . ." Brynne protested.

"I can bring it round tomorrow, miss," Donald said quickly, "if ye dinna' mind givin' me a ride home later, that is."

"Driving back in daylight would make a lot more sense than driving back tonight," Margaret agreed wholeheartedly.

"That's settled, then," Ross said quickly, not giving Brynne another chance to speak.

Margaret got their coats out of the hall closet, and Ross helped Brynne into hers. She felt his hands rest on her shoulders for just a brief moment as she pulled on the coat. It shocked her to feel a tremor of desire run down her spine.

What would it feel like, she wondered, if his hands caressed her bare skin?

They ran through the driving rain to the car. When Brynne sat down on the leather bucket seat, she shook the water from her hair, brushing back damp tendrils that clung to her cheeks. Her mackintosh was wet just from the brief seconds it took to run the few feet from the house to the car. She took it off, laying it on the floor of the car, where it sat in a wet crumpled heap beneath her feet.

Ross got in and started the engine. It was a powerful car and it drove smoothly through the fierce storm.

Though Brynne could see almost nothing through the darkness and the heavy rain, she stared ahead determinedly. She was trying not to think about Ross, how near he was, the pleasant scent of his after-shave. He was a good driver and he guided the car easily on the slippery road.

Brynne stole a glance at his hands on the wheel, the fingers long and slender, the knuckles white from gripping the wheel firmly. They were sensitive hands, and despite herself, Brynne found herself imagining what they would feel like on her body.

But that thought was much too dangerous. Brynne tried to think of something else: the painting she had begun that day, the renovations on the castle, which were nearly complete now . . .

"I've been thinking about you all week," Ross said abruptly. Though his voice was low and soft, it broke the silence of the small, enclosed world that the two of them were sharing on this stormy night.

Suddenly Brynne felt like a teenager again, embarrassed and excruciatingly ill-at-ease. To her chagrin, she handled the situation as awkwardly as any teenager. She responded with a barely audible "Oh?"

Ross glanced at her swiftly, then looked once more at the winding road.

This is ridiculous, Brynne thought, angry at herself as well as at Ross for making her feel this way. I won't play these games.

"Why did you come back?" she asked.

"To see *you*, of course. I thought that was perfectly clear."

"I told you how I feel. I don't want to be involved with anyone."

"Yes, you told me. In no uncertain terms. You might as well put up a sign—'Do Not Touch.' The only problem is, that isn't how you really feel. You know that as well as I do."

"What makes you think you know me better than I know myself? You've only seen me a few times."

"But I've kissed you twice," Ross replied, shooting her a quick look once more. "You can protest all you want, Brynne; the fact is, the woman I held in my arms is capable of feeling passion. Your body couldn't lie."

She was all the more angry because he was right. Clenching her hands furiously, she retorted, "What's wrong, Ross—can't your ego take the fact that a woman might not want you? Are you so used to willing barmaids at the local taverns that you don't recognize plain rejection when you see it?"

Her words jolted his confidence. She could see that by the tightening of his mouth and the stiff set of his shoulders. And though part of her regretted her harshness, especially the pain she'd inflicted, another part was triumphant.

They were near the castle now. In a moment, Ross turned the car into the short drive that led down to it from the main road. Brynne noticed that his hands gripped the steering wheel even more tightly now, with anger.

"If you're so interested in my sexual history, I'll tell you—I've never bedded a barmaid in my life. You won't drive me away by insulting me, Brynne."

He stopped the car in front of the castle, turning off the engine and the lights. In the darkness, Brynne could barely make out the expression on his face. But she sensed both his anger and his passion.

"Dammit Brynne, I want you! You can say all you want about how short a time we've known each other. I've told myself the same thing, over and over. But the argument falls apart when I think about you. You stir me in a way no woman has ever done before! And you can deny it till doomsday, but I know I do the same to you."

He pulled her toward him and kissed her deeply, stifling her brief, halfhearted protest with his searing kiss and powerful embrace. She responded with all the pent-up passion that she had tried so hard to deny. Her arms went around his neck, lightly touching the short, soft hairs that curled around his collar.

When he finally released her, he looked at her, his pale eyes so full of love and desire that Brynne felt her heart melt. His level, penetrating gaze seemed to touch her in some vital, undiscovered place. She had never felt this way before, even at the height of passion with Allen. And it frightened her.

In the intimacy of the darkness in the small, enclosed car, they might have been the only two people in the world.

With the softest touch of his fingertips, he traced her eyes, her lips, the line of her jaw. This sensual movement was the lightest touch, yet it held her with the surest strength.

"'Tis useless to deny it. What we feel for each other is real," Ross insisted, his voice a hoarse whisper.

But Brynne was terrified by the intensity of her feelings, shaken by the thought of losing herself once more just when she was beginning to find herself. For the first time in her life, she was in control, doing exactly as she pleased. But with Ross, she knew, she was perilously close to losing all control. Her desire for him was so overpowering that she felt like a butterfly besieged by a bull.

Desperately she tried to explain her feelings to him. "In love, one person devours and the other is devoured. If I let myself love you, it will be the end of me as a free individual standing on my own. I won't have that, Ross. I won't belong to anyone, body or soul, again. At least not yet. Not when everything is still so tentative and fragile."

She saw immediately that he didn't understand, wouldn't even try to.

"I've lain awake for six nights thinking of you, wanting you. You can't tell me you haven't felt the same longing."

"Ross, I won't argue with you. I *can't*. I *must* go," she finished desperately.

Quickly she opened the door and ran from the car, leaving her coat behind. Despite the rain and the tears that blinded her eyes, she made her way through the courtyard to the front door. Rummaging in her purse, she found the key and unlocked the door. But as she was about to step across the threshold into warmth and safety, she stopped.

Powerful emotions raged within her as she stood there, dripping wet. She was torn between her intense desire for this man who wouldn't leave her in peace, and her new-found, fragile freedom.

Love won.

Slowly she turned and looked back the way she had come, at the car that still sat quietly, a white ghost in the darkness. The door on the driver's side opened. Slowly, purposefully, a dark figure came through the pounding rain toward her. He stopped only inches from her. His wet hair clung to his head.

She met his eyes' level gaze—those piercing, not-quite-green eyes that had seen past her fragile defenses to the hunger beneath.

"Surrender, my sweetest lass," he urged huskily. "Even the walls of this castle couldn't keep you from me tonight."

My sweetest lass . . . The words from my dream! Brynne thought wonderingly.

What little resistance that remained, crumbled then, as Ross swept her up into his arms and carried her into the castle.

Chapter Ten

*H*e carried her, wet and shivering from more than the cold, up the stone steps to the second floor, and then into her bedroom. Outside, the storm raged, the rain beating insistently against the tall windows. But inside it was utterly quiet and still.

He let her down in the bathroom, on the soft, shaggy rug in front of the big claw-footed tub. Turning on the hot water, he added some scented bath oil that sat on a nearby counter.

Then he turned to face Brynne. One by one, he undid the row of tiny buttons on the front of her dripping-wet dress. Then he pulled the garment down past her shoulders and hips, letting it fall to the floor in a damp, crumpled heap. She stepped out of it gingerly, at the same time kicking off her camel-colored leather pumps. Then Ross undid the clasp of the white silk teddy that clung wetly to her skin. In a moment, that too had fallen to the floor, and Brynne stood naked and shivering before him.

Quickly he shed his own clothes, stepping out of his slacks, discarding his shirt, emerging slim and taut, every muscle shuddering with the cold.

The tub was half-full of warm water now, and he turned off the faucet. Picking Brynne up, he set her down gently in the water, then followed her. Facing her, he began to lather her entire body with a bar of jasmine-scented soap. The warm, slippery feeling of his hands working their way down from her shoulders to her breasts, and then to her stomach, was the most sensuous experience she'd ever had. She felt drunk with the heady sensations of the hot water, the scent of jasmine, and the feel of his hands, gentle yet firm, roving over her.

Quickly he brought warmth to her ice-cold skin. It was an intimacy so exquisite it was almost painful in its intensity.

He washed her trembling breasts, moving in slow, sensuous circles, lingering over nipples that were hard with desire. Brynne leaned back against the smooth porcelain of the tub and half-closed her eyes as Ross continued the warm, wet massage of her body.

His hands moved down to her flat stomach, continuing their erotic circular motion. Warmth suffused her, and when she trembled now, it wasn't from the cold.

When he was through, Brynne took the bar of soap and did the same to him. Lightly she caressed his shoulders, his neck, his broad, smooth chest. The bath oil in the water made her fingers glide smoothly over his skin. Her long, slow strokes aroused him, and she could see by the smoldering light in his eyes how much he wanted her.

When her fingertips reached his flat stomach, her touch became lighter. It wasn't time yet to explore him intimately. That, she knew, would come later.

When the bath was over, Ross stepped out of the tub, then helped Brynne out. Taking a large towel from a hook nearby, he began drying her. The towel felt so soft as it moved over her, making her body tingle.

When she was dry, he took another towel and dried himself quickly, running the towel up and down over his rippling muscles and sinewy limbs. Brynne watched him, unashamed of her own nakedness and frankly curious about his body. For days now she had thought about him, fleetingly, with a guilty conscience for her traitorous thoughts. Now she felt no guilt, only a profound desire.

Ross led her into the bedroom, then bent to start a fire. In a moment Brynne felt the warmth of the small, growing flames, and heard the brisk crackle of the dry wood as it was consumed by fire. Ross rose and smiled at Brynne gently. She returned the smile, happy now, at peace within herself, no longer fighting the desire she felt for him. She wanted what they were about to share.

He led her to the bed, and they lay down in it together.

"I've wanted you so long . . . it almost

seems like forever," Ross said, his voice velvety soft. His hazel eyes were filled with the wonder of her, naked and welcoming beside him.

"You could have taken me anytime. My resistance was entirely superficial," Brynne confessed.

"If only I'd known . . ." Ross replied, that familiar crooked grin softening his face. "Do you mean I didn't need a jasmine-scented bath, a romantic fire and a comfortable bed?"

"No. It's shameless of me to admit it, but where you're concerned, a carpet of grass and the open sky would be enough."

She ran one fingertip lightly over his broad shoulders and down the hard muscles of his arm. At her touch, a tremor of desire ran through his body.

Looking at her intently, he asked, "Are you afraid?"

"A little," she admitted honestly. "I don't know what it will be like. I'm excited and a little nervous. Will you be happy with me? I wonder. Will things be as perfect as I want them to be for you?"

"The answers are simple, love. You make me happier than I've ever felt in my life." He finished huskily, "And I promise you, it will be perfect."

His reassurance was all she needed to relax completely and give herself to him without reservations.

He made love to her as no man had ever done before. With Allen, lovemaking had been tender and sweet. With Ross it was an erotic adventure. He made her wildest, most privately held fantasies come true as he made love to her totally, imaginatively, perfectly. His caresses were fluid. He kissed and softly stroked every inch of her body. He kissed her in unexpected places—the palms of her hands, between her fingers, the small of her back—and brought her shivers of delight.

His lips were warm and moist, his tongue was an erotic delight. With it he probed her mouth, touching the highly sensitive roof. He lightly circled her ear with his tongue, making quick in-and-out movements.

When he blew lightly in her ear, she shuddered with desire and pressed herself closer to him. She wanted to feel the hard length of his body against her, skin meeting skin.

Brynne didn't want to lie there passively. She wanted to give him the same pleasure he was giving her. As his lips continued their journey of exploration over her body, she began kissing him and biting him provocatively. With a feather-light touch she ran her fingertips across the tiny soft hairs at the small of his back and up his spine. She massaged his back and shoulders, pulling him closer to her, and blew light, short breaths onto his skin.

"I want you so," she whispered.

"My sweetest lass," he responded, covering her with kisses—her face, the hollow at the base of her throat, her full, trembling breasts.

When his tongue circled her rose-red nipples, she moaned with pleasure. And when his lips traveled even farther down her body, she clutched at his shoulders with a fevered grip. As his fingertips stroked her gently rounded hips and soft derriere, he kissed her in the most intimate part of her, his lips soft, his tongue warm and moist against her tender flesh.

Brynne thrust her hips upward, offering herself to Ross. His movements were teasing, elusive now, and she began to feel she couldn't wait another moment for the ultimate fulfillment.

"Please," she whispered, pleading.

The word seemed to galvanize him. He looked up at her erotic eyes and wet lips. Then slowly, with infinite gentleness, he moved on top of her, his hard chest pressing down on her breasts, her ivory-skinned stomach heaving under him, her hips against his.

Now she felt not only her own turmoil but his as well as they bonded, partaking of each other in total intimacy. They rolled across the bed in tight embrace, clutching, folding, all curves filled. Waves of desire coursed through Brynne. Her cries, soft at first, mounted in endless spirals, widening, expanding, become more uninhibited.

And then, like fireworks going off, a shower of white-hot ecstasy spread through her body just as he shuddered against her violently.

For a long time they lay quietly together, her cheek nestled against his smooth chest, watching the firelight dancing on the walls. It reminded Brynne of something . . . something buried deep in her conscious-ness that wouldn't quite come clear. Words flitted through her mind . . . moonlight, shadows . . .

Then slowly, word by word, it came to her . . .

On my garden wall,
   moonlight traces patterns
   of yesterday's sweet bouquet.
Then, genestra, satin-glossed
   and yellow-bright,
   swayed on slender stems
   and danced partners
   with a gentle wind.
Now, in this quiet night,
   my heart calls
   to yesterday when love was—
   and shadows did not pattern
   on my garden wall.

Somehow, Brynne knew the poem was connected with Laurie. Whether Laurie had simply read it somewhere, or written it herself, or perhaps only shared the emotions in it, wasn't important. All that mattered was that Brynne and Ross's passion was centuries old. It had flamed once between Laurie and Richard, and was now reborn for her and Ross.

Suddenly Ross stirred. Looking down at Brynne, he asked gently, "What is it, love? You look so pensive."

"I was just thinking about shadows."

"You mean the firelight?"

"Yes. And other shadows . . . from the past."

"I don't understand," he responded idly, kissing her forehead and pulling her closer against him.

"In Carmel I felt that I was constantly in

Allen's shadow as an artist. That's why I couldn't paint there. I'd always be compared to him. Here I feel that what you and I share is somehow overshadowed by Laurie and Richard's tragic love."

Ross rose on one arm and gazed down at her, surprised. "How did you know the Lord of the Isles's name was Richard?" he asked, puzzled. "That wasn't in my book."

Brynne thought for a long moment. Finally she said slowly, "I don't know. I just knew somehow that it was."

"Perhaps Donald mentioned it when he was telling you about the legend."

"Perhaps."

As Ross looked down at her, nestled in the crook of his arm, he smiled that engaging crooked grin and said softly, "At least you've stopped fighting me. You're a very stubborn lass, Brynne McAllister."

"Did you ever have any doubt you would win in the end?" Brynne asked teasingly.

"At first, I admit I did, a bit. You were so determined to resist me, to deny what was between us. But now . . ." Once more his finger traced her jawline, pausing just under the chin to lift her face so that he was looking directly into her eyes. "I don't believe the legend of Laurie Fraser has anything to do with us. The past is dead and gone. What's between us now is all that matters."

As he took Brynne in his arms, she thought: Perhaps he's right. This moment is all that matters. And this moment is ours.

But as she fell asleep with his arm around her protectively, something in her, remembering, looked back into the past . . . and she felt as if she were falling inexorably into a dark, timeless wasteland of loneliness. . . .

Laurie threw back the coverlet and, still naked, walked softly across the carpet to the open window. It wasn't yet daylight, not yet time for Richard to leave. He was so busy with the king nowadays that she saw him only for brief, stolen moments.

But right now the sky was still gray, not yet rosy pink, and he was hers for a while longer. She shivered. It was cold at this early hour. Quickly she returned to the bed, to his body, lying warm and naked.

He opened his eyes and smiled at her. But there was something in the smile, a sadness, that had never been there before. She had sensed from the moment he walked in that this time was subtly different. Their private world of peace and love had been broken somehow. Forcing her mind to clear from the mists of their lovemaking, Laurie asked, "Why did the king keep you so late?"

"We're to march on the English," Richard answered bluntly. "'Twill be the end o' the bloody sassenachs, finally. Scotland will stand proud an' free." Suddenly raising up on one arm, he looked at her intently and finished, "Come wi' me, Laurie, to Falkland Palace. There's time enough for us to be married before I leave. Then, when 'tis over, I'll come back to ye, my wife."

She rose, reluctantly leaving the comfort of his strong arms, and lit a candle. Then she found her dressing gown and put it on.

"Ye ken how I feel, Richard," she said firmly. The words were softened by love, but there was a finality to them. It was this stubbornness that he found at once irritating and appealing in her.

"For once, let go o' yer damned pride!" he urged angrily, throwing off the blanket and taking her in his arms. "Be *mine*, love."

"I've given ye my body an' my heart. Isn't that enough?"

"No!"

"Is it the Fraser lands, then, that ye want?" she asked angrily. Immediately she regretted the unfair accusation.

His pale eyes went cold. "Remember who yer talkin' to, Laurie. I'm the Lord of the Isles, an' I've wealth enough for any man. I dunna' covet your holdings. I want *you*."

"But only on *your* terms?" she lashed back.

"My God, 'tis considered an honor, no' an insult, to propose marriage! Why do ye insist on bein' so stubborn?"

"Because I willna' be any man's chattel!"

He looked at her for a moment, then rose and strode over to his clothes, lying in a crumpled heap at the foot of the bed.

Soon he was dressed. She watched him, feeling a gnawing fear inside. She'd never driven him this far before, and she was painfully aware that his pride was even greater than hers.

"I'll leave ye now, to think on it. But I'll be waitin' on the hill behind the castle. Decide if ye want to come wi' me, to be my wife. I'll give ye an hour to decide."

As he started to leave, she shouted furiously, "Richard!"

"I've waited long enough, Laurie!" he shot back. "I'll claim ye as my own before God an' the world, or I'll never see ye again."

And then he was gone.

She returned to the bed, pulling the blanket up to her quivering chin. She searched with her cheek for the hollow where his head had lain. The sheet was cold now, but there was still a lingering scent of him.

The moon had set, it was nearly dawn, and the room was utterly dark. She lay there thinking desperately. She'd been mistress of her affairs since her parents both died five years earlier. She was the last of the Frasers of Castle Fraser. There was no one to tell her what to do, to take charge of what was rightfully hers. She made her own decisions, did as she pleased. And when she saw other women living under the iron rule of their husbands or fathers, she breathed a sigh of relief. She was *free*.

And then she had met Richard, and suddenly her heart was no longer her own.

Why is he so determined to wed? she asked herself irritably. They were happy as they were, and neither cared what the wagging tongues of gossips might say. But deep inside she recognized what drove him to possess her in the eyes of the church and the world. He was the Lord of the Isles, used to being master of all he surveyed. He had to know that she was his, completely and forever.

If she gave in to him, married him as he

wished, everything that belonged to her would go to him. He would control her life in every way and she would no longer be free. Only his love for her was guarantee of his good treatment of her—as long as that love should last.

Sighing, she clenched her fists angrily. She had to choose between her freedom and her love for him. She could not have both. But loneliness was a high price to pay for freedom. Without him, life would be empty and meaningless.

"Richard, my love," she whispered to the darkness. Already the room seemed cold and barren without him.

Her heart made the decision for her.

She rose and dressed hurriedly. She didn't know the time, but surely, she thought, it couldn't have been much more than an hour since he'd stalked out. He would still be waiting for her—he *must* still be waiting.

She threw on a cloak, then ran out of the castle. The sky was gray, dew was on the ground, and the drenched grass was shimmering under the faint morning stars. It was cold in this godforsaken hour just before dawn. Shivering, Laurie pulled the cloak more tightly around her as she ran through the wet grass. A cock crowed nearby. There was a slight rustle in the trees; a badger, perhaps, or a deer.

Laurie looked up eagerly toward the hill that rose gently behind the castle. But it was still too dark to see anything.

Vividly she remembered his last words to her: "I'll wait one hour, no more."

She ran faster, pulling up her long skirt, breathing harder as she climbed the hill.

But when she reached the crest and looked around, it was deserted. He had gone.

"Richard!" she called into the gray early dawn. But there was no answer. . . .

Brynne awoke with a start. Turning, she saw Ross wide-awake, watching her softly.

"Ross!" There was fear and confusion in that one whispered word.

"What is it, lass? You look so frightened."

"I . . . I had a bad dream. You were gone and I couldn't find you and there was only an endless eternity of loneliness in front of me."

Her lips trembled and tears glistened at the corners of her eyes.

Smiling gently, Ross pulled her against him. "Hush, now, love, there's nothing to worry about. I'll never leave you, Brynne."

But as she nestled in the crook of his arm, she felt a lingering fear. The dream had seemed so real.

Chapter Eleven

*B*rynne went into Kirkcudbright early Monday morning to pick up Jane. The train pulled up to the platform and Brynne scanned the crowd for her sister. Finally she spotted Jane, loaded down with packages and looking tired but happy.

"How was the trip?" Brynne asked cheerfully, helping Jane with her packages.

"Marvelous! Edinburgh's *gorgeous*. You've got to go up there sometime."

"Perhaps I will," Brynne replied with a secret smile. Then she added, "You seem to have bought out the town."

"Nearly. Well, I hadn't spent any money in a month and my wallet was beginning to feel awfully heavy."

"What did you do besides shop?" Brynne

asked as they piled Jane's packages into the trunk of the car.

"Ate, mostly. The pubs have the most wonderful food. Plain but delicious. I got a recipe for a terrific meat pie. And I saw a couple of movies, both bad. Let's have tea before we go home, and I'll tell you all about it."

They went into a nearby tea shop and ordered tea and scones. Brynne was getting to like the dark Scottish tea, but Jane still insisted on watering hers down to the thin consistency Americans are used to.

After talking about Edinburgh for several minutes, Jane asked curiously, "What did *you* do while I was gone?"

"Oh, this and that," Brynne replied evasively. "I finished a painting of that old cobbled close where Donald has his office. I'm very happy with it."

"Stop," Jane said, holding up her hand expressively. "I don't want to hear that you buried yourself in your painting all weekend."

"Actually, I didn't," Brynne replied. She enjoyed teasing Jane. Then she added with studied casualness, "I went to a party at Donald's Saturday night."

"That must have been wild," Jane replied dryly. But something in Brynne's expression caught her attention. "Wait a minute. You look pleased with yourself for some reason. And excited. What exactly happened at this party, anyway?"

"Nothing, really," Brynne answered noncommittally as the waitress brought scones and jam and set them on the table. When she left, Brynne continued, "It was a small dinner, just Donald and Margaret . . . and Ross Fleming."

"Oh . . ." Jane said, drawing out the word speculatively. Looking intently at Brynne now, she finished, "I see."

"Do you?" Brynne asked.

"Yes, I do. Brynne, you sly rascal, why didn't you tell me? Here I've been prattling on about shopping and food, and you've gone and fallen in love!"

"Jane!" Brynne said loudly, then lowered her voice as the other people in the small tea shop looked at her curiously. "Who said anything about falling in love? I merely said Ross was at the party."

"And you slept with him and you're head-over-heels in love."

"How on earth can you jump to such a conclusion?" Brynne asked, astounded.

"It's easy. I should have seen it the moment I laid eyes on you. You look different, all sparkly and alive in a way you haven't done for months."

Brynne smiled, acknowledging Jane's perception. "But *nothing* was said about love."

"Then you're both wasting time. Why not admit you love each other and get it over with?"

"Jane, you're impossible. I haven't known Ross long enough to love him. And *you've* only seen him once. How can you assume he loves me?"

"Because it was obvious that night he came to the castle for dinner. He couldn't take his eyes off you. If ever a man was smitten, it was he. You can deny it till hell freezes over, but I know you love him, too."

"Do you think you're picking up some of Donald's famous 'second sight'?"

"Maybe." Jane laughed, then continued, "I'm your sister, remember. I know you better than you know yourself in some ways."

"You and Ross have that in common," Brynne said wryly. "It seems everyone else in the world knows me better than I know myself. At least, you all *think* you do."

"So, tell me about him. Not what he's like in bed. I'm sure he's fantastic, or you wouldn't be looking so content."

Brynne laughed. "All right. I'll give you the less-intimate details. The bottom line is, he's *nice*."

"Not an arrogant, stubborn philanderer?" Jane said, mischievously quoting Brynne's earlier assessment of Ross.

"Um, well, he *is* a bit arrogant," Brynne admitted, sipping her tea slowly. "And more than a bit stubborn. But he's also intelligent and witty and sensitive."

"In other words, a real catch."

"I'm not interested in marriage," Brynne said flatly. After taking a bite of scone, she added, "And he knows that."

"Does he, now?" Jane asked, cocking her head to one side and eyeing her sister curiously.

"I'm serious, Jane," Brynne continued soberly. "I have no intention of giving up my new life and my career just to polish someone else's glory. I want my own glory."

"Can't you have both? Can't you be Mrs.

Ross Fleming *and* pursue your painting?
Money wouldn't be a problem this time."

Brynne paused before answering thoughtfully, "No, but a lot of other things would.
Ross, like most men, likes getting his way.
And I'm not in a mood to be accommodating
nowadays. Besides, he hasn't asked me to
marry him."

"He will," Jane insisted confidently as she
finished the last of her tea. Setting down the
white china cup on the blue-flowered table-
cloth, she added, "Ross Fleming doesn't strike
me as the sort of man who hesitates to take
what he wants when he finds it."

"He's also the sort who would demand a
great deal from his wife. At this point, I'm not
prepared to play hostess and provide full-time
emotional support. There'd be no time left for
my own career."

Jane's expression had grown more serious.
"Brynne, it doesn't necessarily have to be the
way it was with Allen. Ross is a different
person."

"I know that. I'm not confusing the two of
them," Brynne said thoughtfully. After a moment she continued, "But there are certain
underlying realities that are fairly constant.
It's hard for two big egos to live in harmony."

"But you don't have a big ego," Jane responded quickly.

"Oh, Janey, it's hard to explain. I just have
this awful certainty that Ross could overpow-
er me if I let him."

"Has he used that power over you?"

"Not yet."

"Maybe he never will."

"*Maybe*. I can't count on that, though."

Brynne finished her tea quickly and said briskly, "But enough of this. I didn't intend to get into such a serious discussion so soon. Let's stop at the post office and pick up our mail, then go on to the castle. I'm dying to show you what I've done."

"Okay," Jane agreed. But she couldn't resist adding, "Just don't guard your heart *too* closely, Brynne."

Brynne looked at her intently but said nothing.

They got their mail from the post office. As Brynne drove away from Kirkcudbright, Jane scanned the thick batch of magazines, catalogs and letters. Suddenly she stopped, remaining utterly motionless for several long seconds as she stared at a letter. Glancing over at her, Brynne asked, "What's wrong?"

After a moment, Jane replied softly, without looking at Brynne, "It's from Todd."

Her voice was stunned, disbelieving, yet filled with immense relief. At that moment Brynne realized what it had cost Jane not to contact her lover. She saw how desperately Jane had missed him. She muttered a distressed "Damn!" under her breath.

Why couldn't he leave Jane alone? she asked herself.

Jane said nothing more for the rest of the drive. When they got to the castle, she went directly to her bedroom.

Brynne went into her studio and tried to work on a painting of a willow tree whose branches trailed in the water of the small stream near the castle. But her mind was on Jane, not her work.

After several minutes, Jane came into the studio, holding the letter in her hand. Her face was suffused with a kind of happiness that Brynne hadn't seen since they left Carmel.

Putting down her brush and palette, Brynne waited expectantly.

"He wants me to call him," Jane said in answer to Brynne's unasked question. "He misses me terribly."

"And *you* miss him," Brynne said softly. "Until today, I didn't realize how much you've missed him."

"I tried not to think about him, but it was impossible," Jane responded, unable to control a growing excitement in her voice. "I know how you feel about this, Brynne. But I love him. And try as I will, I can't seem to get over that."

"I just don't want to see you get hurt. Janey, it's a rotten situation—you're the mistress of a man who's married, who has children. You can't expect anything from him but heartbreak."

"I know," Jane whispered, her voice small and helpless. Gone was the confident, happy young woman Brynne had always known. In her place was a woman caught up in a love that was tearing her apart.

"Are you going to call him?" Brynne asked though she knew the answer.

"I *must*. I have to know what he wants to talk to me about. I'm sorry, Brynne," she finished confusedly, then turned and left the room.

"Damn!" Brynne said, this time loudly and angrily.

She was so angry about the situation that she decided not to talk to Jane about it again unless Jane brought up the subject herself. She felt a tremendous temptation to tell Jane to grow up, to look at things honestly, to show some of her old spunk instead of buckling under to this man whom Brynne disliked intensely even though she'd never met him.

But she knew that would be exactly the wrong attitude to take with her stubborn younger sister. As difficult as it was, all she could do was wait to see what happened, and be there for Jane when she needed a shoulder to cry on.

Days passed, and Jane said nothing of her conversation with Todd. But she seemed happier than she had in a month, and she radiated an expectant excitement.

Then on Friday Ross returned to Fleming House. He had called Brynne twice during the week, and they agreed that he would come to Castle Fraser for dinner Friday night. Brynne wanted Ross and Jane—the two people she cared most about in the world—to get to know and like each other.

Jane and Ross got along well from the start. Jane teased him in her old impudent way, and they had a long conversation about cuisine in Edinburgh. Ross was something of a gourmet and he told Jane about many restaurants she should try when she was in Edinburgh next.

After dinner, Brynne offered to straighten up the kitchen, since Jane had prepared the meal.

"I'll help," Ross offered.

"No, it'll only take a few minutes. One of the things I had Donald install was a dishwasher. You and Jane go into the living room and I'll join you soon."

They left, and as Brynne worked, she heard the low rumble of conversation as Ross and Jane talked.

After a few minutes, Brynne joined them for coffee and brandy. The three of them stayed up long past midnight discussing many things. Finally Ross said, "I'd better be going. I know you'll want to work tomorrow, Brynne."

He rose and said good-bye to Jane.

"It was nice meeting you again, Ross," Jane replied warmly. "I'm sure we'll be seeing a lot of you."

She flashed a quick grin at Brynne, who ignored her.

As Brynne walked outside with Ross, she felt the stillness of the warm summer night. The trees stood motionless, and not a creature stirred in the darkness. Ross put his arm around her waist as they walked up to his car.

"What did you and Jane talk about in my absence?" Brynne asked curiously.

"You, of course," he answered, smiling. "She asked me what my intentions are toward you."

"She didn't."

"She did indeed. She's a very straightforward young lady. I like her. But I like *you* better," he finished, kissing Brynne's forehead affectionately.

"Keep to the subject," Brynne admonished, smiling. "What did you tell her your intentions are? Strictly dishonorable?"

"On the contrary." His expression changed, growing more serious. "I've thought about you all week, Brynne. I want to make love to you, 'tis true. But I also want more than that."

"Ross . . ." Brynne started to interrupt.

"No, let me finish. I'm not a boy, Brynne, out for conquests. I'm thirty-five years old, and I know my own mind and heart. This isn't just another affair as far as I'm concerned. I want you to know that."

Brynne said nothing. Her mind was in turmoil.

Why can't it be simple? she wondered unhappily. Why does something so wonderful have to be so complicated?

"Come to Fleming House for dinner tomorrow night," Ross urged as he opened his car door. "And bring a toothbrush. I want to hold you in my arms again, all night long. No more of this kissing you good night at your door."

Brynne laughed softly, looking seductively up at Ross through thick lashes. "All right. I'll tell Jane not to wait up for me."

In what was becoming a familiar habit, Ross ran one finger lightly around her face, tracing the outline of her jaw and stopping at her chin. He lifted her chin so that her eyes were looking up into his.

"Till tomorrow, love."

He kissed her deeply, lingeringly, filling her body with a sweet, aching longing. She wanted him intensely, then and there. Waiting twenty-four hours would be awful.

She watched as he drove off, and continued standing there until the white Porsche was out of sight.

Chapter Twelve

*B*rynne was packing a small overnight bag the next night, and Jane was lying on the bed watching her. Jane was humming under her breath the not-too-subtle song "Love Is a Many-Splendored Thing."

"All right," Brynne said firmly, turning to face Jane. "Why don't you just say what's on your mind?"

Jane gave her a look of calculated innocence. "I don't know what on earth you're talking about."

"Janey, when a thirty-one-year-old woman chooses to spend the night with a thirty-five-year-old man, it doesn't necessarily mean love and marriage."

"Of course not," Jane agreed easily. "After all, you do this sort of thing all the time."

147

Brynne grabbed a small pillow and threw it at her sister in mock anger.

"For a woman who's only out for a romp in the hay, you're certainly touchy on the subject," Jane said, placing the pillow behind her head and resting on it placidly.

"Why do you insist on reading so much into my relationship with Ross?" Brynne asked, sitting down on the edge of the bed.

"It's obvious you love each other. I don't know why you're fighting it so."

"Did he tell you that when you talked alone last night?" Brynne couldn't resist asking.

"*See,* you're not nearly as blasé as you pretend," Jane said triumphantly, rolling over onto her side and smiling at Brynne. "As a matter of fact, he didn't actually say he loved you. But he asked me about Allen, and whether or not I thought you were still in love with him."

"And what did you tell him?"

"That you loved Allen very much but had put that part of your life behind you now. I told him not to be put off by your stubborn independence and pride. He said he likes those qualities in you—up to a point."

"You seem to have had quite a nice little chat about me."

"Yes, we did," Jane replied, ignoring the sarcasm in Brynne's voice. "He's a terrific guy, Brynne. You're lucky to meet a man who values you for just what you are. He doesn't want you to change to please him. Admit how rare that is, and admit that you love him."

"But I wouldn't be an easy person to live with now," Brynne replied defensively, thinking about how much she'd changed lately. She was engrossed in her painting in a way she'd never been before. She knew her own mind and was firm about things being done the way she wanted them.

Even Donald had commented on her determination once when they'd disagreed about something he was doing to the castle. Politely but firmly, Brynne had insisted on having it done her way.

Now she explained to Jane, "I'm just too independent."

"That's Ross's problem, if he chooses to take it on. From the looks of him, I'd say he could handle just about anything you cared to dish out."

"We're *both* too independent. And stubborn. And wrapped up in our careers. You know what they say about two-career marriages. If you were me, would you want that kind of marriage?"

"No. It's too complicated. There's too much chance of an explosion with two temperaments like yours. You both care so much about your careers."

"That's just it. I'm coming into my own now, both as an artist and as a person. I don't want to risk losing myself again in someone else. With Allen I simply gave in completely and put his needs and wants above my own. But I can't do that again. With Ross, it would be a constant battle of wills. And that would be exhausting."

"Then end the relationship," Jane said flatly. "It's either that or accept the challenge of having him in your life. Because, believe me,

Brynne, that man is *not* going to be put off easily."

Later, as Brynne drove to Fleming House, she tried to put Jane's blunt words out of her mind. She wanted to be with Ross, to know the exquisite joys of making love to him, to enjoy his fascinating conversation, to share her work with him. But she didn't want to give that essential part of herself, the very center of her being. Not yet. Not until she was more sure of herself.

The butler served dinner on the terrace. Summer in Scotland brings incredibly long and beautiful twilights. The long, softly lighted evening was filled with elongated shadows. The world was suddenly strange, romantic, full of seductive charm, a paradise for lovers. The setting sun didn't beat down, it distilled its warmth and its beauty gently for long hours.

Brynne sat across from Ross at a small, white-cloth-covered table. On it were the antique family silver, polished to a shine, and gleaming china in a chinoiserie pattern of bold red, green, blue and yellow. Everything was perfect—the chilled white wine in a silver bucket, the roast leg of lamb with mint jelly, and the dessert, cream puffs shaped like swans, filled with thick, heavy cream.

As they ate and drank, Brynne and Ross talked easily, unselfconsciously, about a myriad of subjects—Ross's fall list of books, interesting authors he knew, Brynne's paintings, amusing incidents in local politics.

Yet beneath the friendly banter was something more—an awareness of the night that was slowly descending upon them; a knowledge of what the darkness would bring. They had made love all throughout that stormy night a week earlier. They knew each other's bodies intimately now. That knowledge made what was to come even more exciting. Each knew what gave the other pleasure, and they looked forward to that pleasure-giving.

We're at a wonderful point in our relationship, Brynne thought contentedly. We want to tell each other everything, to experience every form of pleasure with each other. We can't say enough, do enough, give enough. All the time in the world seems hardly long enough to know each other as well as we want to.

As the evening shadows lengthened, she looked at Ross with undisguised desire. After dinner, they lingered over coffee, but neither wanted brandy. They didn't want what was to come to be dulled in any way.

Finally the night came and the only light was the soft, flickering candlelight from the tall silver candlesticks in the center of the table.

Their conversation died down to an expectant silence. Ross reached across the table to where Brynne's hand lay. Taking her slender hand in his larger one, he said in a husky whisper, "Come, love."

He rose, and she followed as he led her into the house. They passed through the large formal drawing room and into the hall, where a broad, curving staircase led up to the second story.

Ross's bedroom was huge. One end had a white marble fireplace flanked by a sofa and two chairs. A large desk sat in front of a mullioned window. At the other end, a massive bed covered with a chocolate-brown velvet spread sat on a raised dais, with two steps leading up to it.

It was an entirely masculine room, decorated with heavy antiques, upholstered in shades of brown. Brass bowls full of bronze chrysanthemums were the only note of brightness. Even the thick Aubusson carpet was in shades of gold and brown.

On this beautiful summer evening there was no need for a fire. The tall mullioned windows were open, letting in the most imperceptible breeze.

As they stood by the bed, Ross began to unbutton the white camisole top that Brynne wore over a matching full skirt. She reached up, covering his hand with her smaller one, stopping him.

"No, Ross. Tonight it's my turn to make love to you."

She glanced seductively up at him and flashed a wicked smile. Slowly his mouth broke into a grin of surprise and delight.

"Very well. I'm in your hands," he said, his hazel eyes shining with anticipation.

First, she undressed him. She took off the tan linen jacket he was wearing, then unbuttoned the mint-green silk shirt. For a moment she paused, running her fingertips lightly across his smooth, broad chest. Then she continued, unbuckling the belt of his tan slacks. When her hands brushed his hard, flat stomach, she felt his muscles contract in a spasm of desire. In a moment, he was naked.

Then, as he stood watching her expectantly, she undressed herself, doing a slow, sensuous striptease for him. With delicious deliberation she undid the buttons on her camisole, one by one. Then she untied the drawstring waist, letting the camisole fall open just enough to reveal the deep valley between her breasts, and the rounded sides of the breasts themselves.

In one fluid movement she slipped off her skirt, with its elasticized waist, letting it fall to the floor at her feet. Now she was wearing only the half-open camisole and the tiniest bikini panties, lace-edged, peach-colored. Then the camisole and the panties lay on the floor with her skirt and the gold sandals she had kicked off.

All Brynne wore now was a thin gold chain that glistened against the pale ivory of her skin.

"Lie down, please," she ordered Ross softly.

Smiling, he complied.

"Tonight is for you, darling," she continued.

As he lay on his back, she knelt over his body. With her knees and feet on the bed, outside his sinewy thighs, she lay astride him, facing him. Slowly, provocatively, she began doing to him all the things he had done to her their first night together. She licked, stroked, kissed every part of his body. She touched the hard muscles at the sides of his neck and twined her fingers through his hair.

He began to shiver with pleasure. The smell and feel of him excited Brynne, making her hungry for every sensation, every way of knowing him. When she kissed him eagerly, he bit her lips just enough to bring pleasure, not pain. His hands cupped her breasts, caressing her and pushing at the same time. Then they moved down to feel the fullness of her hips.

When she kissed him again, it was passionate, furious, his mouth drinking hers.

Ross's voice was potent, his eyes burning as he whispered her name over and over, "Brynne, my Brynne . . ."

Waves of desire dilated her body, opened it, prepared her to yield. She moved then so that he could take her. Now she felt electrically charged, as each thrust sent currents through her body.

Then the currents came together in an intensity so powerful that she cried out, a tremendous sound of joy, ecstasy and profound pleasure.

Afterward they looked down at their tangled bodies and laughed happily. Brynne moved to lie beside him, and Ross leaned over to turn off the bedside lamp. They lay quietly in the darkness, still catching their breath from their lightning-quick, furious lovemaking.

Then gradually they began to talk, first of the pleasure each got from the other, then of other things.

"I've never felt so free with a man," Brynne admitted with a complete lack of embarrassment.

Ross kissed her gently, with affection now and not passion. "And I've never felt so intimate with a woman. Not just physically, but emotionally. I knew this feeling existed, but I was beginning to doubt that I would ever experience it. Then I met you. And from that first night, when you disappeared so mysteriously, I knew I'd found what I'd been looking for."

"What have you been looking for, Ross?" Brynne asked gently.

"Someone to make me feel that I'm not entirely alone," he answered in a low whisper.

Putting her arm across his chest, Brynne snuggled even closer to him. "You're not alone, darling. I'm here, for as long as you want me."

"I'll want you forever," he responded, holding her tightly as if he would never let her go.

Chapter Thirteen

When Brynne returned to Castle Fraser Monday morning, Jane was waiting for her in the living room. Jane's dark eyes sparkled with tiny points of light, like a handful of diamonds on a black velvet background, and she radiated excitement and happiness.

"I've got to talk to you," she began as Brynne came through the door.

"All right," Brynne agreed. "Just let me put my things away, then I'll be right down."

A few minutes later, she returned to the living room. Somehow, she had a feeling of foreboding. Only one person could produce such an effect in Jane. And Brynne didn't want to think about him.

"Todd called last night. Brynne . . . he asked me to marry him."

"But—"

"I know what you're going to say—but he's already married. That's going to change, though. He's left his wife and is going to file for divorce."

"Oh, Jane," Brynne responded, her voice both stunned and disapproving.

"Brynne, everything's going to be all right," Jane insisted. "He said he's really missed me since I've been gone. He realizes that he wants me to be with him permanently. He wants me to come back to Monterey immediately."

When Brynne said nothing, Jane continued haltingly, her enthusiasm dampened, "Don't you see, it's working out after all. You thought I would be hurt, that he would never offer me anything more than a few stolen hours together. But he wants to *marry* me. Don't you see?" she finished, pleading with Brynne to understand, to be happy for her, to approve.

But Brynne couldn't approve. She said slowly, thoughtfully weighing each word, "I admit I was wrong in thinking he would never offer you anything lasting. But, Janey . . . this is hardly the best basis for a relationship. You're building your happiness on someone else's misery. You say everything will be all right now. For you, perhaps, and Todd. But what about his wife and children? Everything certainly won't be all right for them."

Jane's expression hardened into the old stubbornness that Brynne knew so well. "I thought you would be happy for me," she said coldly. "Obviously I expected too much. We won't talk about it again."

Rising, she started to walk out of the room.

"Jane, please. I didn't mean to hurt you. But—"

"I don't want to talk about it, Brynne." Her voice was flat, final.

After a pause, Brynne asked, "What will you do?"

"I've made a reservation on a flight from Glasgow to San Francisco tomorrow night. There's a train from Kirkcudbright to Glasgow in the morning."

"Jane, I'll be happy to drive you up to Glasgow."

"No, I don't want to inconvenience you. If you could just give me a lift to the station."

"Of course."

"If it's any trouble, I can call a taxi."

"Don't be silly. Of course I'll take you."

Before Brynne could say anything further, Jane left the room.

Dinner that night was silent and strained. Brynne tried to make conversation, but Jane wouldn't respond. Never in all their lives had Brynne felt so estranged from her sister. And she had no idea how to bridge the chasm between them.

By the time they arrived at the train station the next morning, things were only slightly better. The sun was shining hotly and the bay gleamed azure under the clear sky. It was a perfect summer day. But Brynne felt a painful incongruity that her heart could be so heavy when the sun was shining so beautifully.

As she prepared to board the train, Jane hugged Brynne quickly and whispered, "Take care of yourself."

"You, too. I do love you, Janey."

"I know. I'm sorry . . ." She paused uncertainly. "Well, I'm just sorry."

"Call me when you arrive."

"Okay."

"And give Jason my love if you see him."

"I will."

Then Jane was on the train, looking out a window at Brynne, who stood waiting on the platform. Brynne continued waiting until the train had pulled away from the station and the rest of the crowd had dispersed. Finally she turned and slowly walked away, her soft brown eyes blurred with tears.

In early August, when the summer was at its warmest and Kirkcudbright shone pristine and whitewashed beneath clear blue skies, Brynne took some of her paintings into the village. Until then, only Ross and Jane had seen her work. Now it was time, she decided, to get a professional opinion, to learn if her paintings were good enough to sell. Her money was rapidly running out, and she was going to have to start earning a living once more.

She went into the largest art gallery in town. She had been in there often, buying paintings by local artists to decorate Castle Fraser. The gallery was one large room with white walls covered by paintings. In a corner stood an old-fashioned black iron wood-burning stove. On top of it, a brass teakettle emitted tiny puffs of steam. Beside the stove were a round table and comfortable chairs where people could sit and discuss a possible purchase or simply argue about art in general.

Brynne had always liked this place for its unpretentious atmosphere. The owner, a genial middle-aged man named Sean Farren, greeted her warmly.

"Ah, Miss McAllister, 'tis a pleasure to see you again. Where've ye been keepin' yerself all summer?"

"Actually, I've been painting," Brynne explained in a nervous rush. Slow down, she told herself. This isn't the National Gallery and Mr. Farren is a friend. "I was hoping you'd have the time to look at some things I've done," she finished more calmly.

"'Twould be a pleasure," he replied, smiling. "Let's go back to the table. Can I get you a cup of tea, perhaps?"

"No, thank you," Brynne replied. Her stomach was churning with anxiety, and she had absolutely no desire to drink or eat anything.

She followed him to the table by the stove.

"Now, then, just open your portfolio here," he said, indicating the broad tabletop.

With trembling fingers Brynne opened the portfolio and took out the two paintings she had brought. She considered them her best work. If Farren didn't like them, it would be pointless to bother showing him anything else.

"Sit down, lass," Farren said, indicating a nearby chair.

While Brynne sat nervously on the edge of the chair, clutching the arms tightly, Farren sat down opposite her and carefully scrutinized the paintings. One was of the courtyard of the castle, done mainly in neutral tones. It wasn't the painting she was working on that first day when Ross came riding up and invited her to a picnic. That picture had long since been discarded as being not good enough. This one featured the rosy-red glow of dawn on the ancient castle walls. Brynne had risen early for a week to get just the right effect.

The second painting was of an ancient stone bridge that spanned a small river near Fleming House. That one was interesting for its contrasting colors—the pale blue of the sky, the gray of the stone, the deep blue of the river.

Both paintings revealed a deep love of nature, an affinity for things old and time-worn but not defeated.

"Um," Farren said thoughtfully.

"Yes?" Brynne asked quickly.

Farren smiled up at her, his china-blue eyes creasing into laugh lines at the corners. "They're very good. To be frank, they're better than I expected. Somehow, I thought you were an amateur, like so many of the tourists who come here in the summer an' dabble in paintin'. But obviously yer a serious artist."

"Then . . . then you think they're not too bad?" Brynne hazarded hopefully.

"Not bad? As I said, they're very good. They show an interesting perspective. An' you handle the play of light an' shadow especially well. Now, let's get down to business. I assume ye brought them to me in hopes I'd sell them?"

"Yes," Brynne replied. He *likes* them, she thought, elated. He actually *likes* them!

She felt as if a great weight had been lifted from her shoulders. Whatever happened, at least he hadn't rejected her out of hand. In one fell swoop, her confidence in her ability as an artist was justified.

"I work on a consignment basis, of course," Farren explained. "If they sell, you get sixty percent, I get forty. I hang them for a month. If they haven't sold by then, you take them back. I can't give you more time because there are so many local artists, I've hardly room to show even the best of them. But somehow, Miss McAllister, I don't think you have to worry. These will stand a good chance of sellin'."

Brynne could hardly believe what was happening. She was so happy she could barely contain her joy. From somewhere deep inside, however, the businesswoman in her rose up.

"That's fine. You'll frame them, I take it."

He laughed appreciatively at her business sense. "You're not such an innocent at this, after all, I see. Why don't we leave it at this—you frame these two an' we'll price them modestly, about £150 each. If they sell, I'll want more o' yer work an' I'll frame anything else I show for ye."

"Agreed," Brynne said quickly.

"Just one thing. You must agree, in writing, not to undercut me. Ye canna' sell comparable work at a lower price to private parties."

"I understand."

"Fine." He rose and shook Brynne's hand heartily. "'Tis a deal, then. I'll send round a contract in the next post. As soon as you sign it an' get it back to me, you can come in an' hang yer work."

"Oh, Mr. Farren, thank you. Thank you *so* much!"

"'Tis my pleasure, Miss McAllister. I'll look forward to seein' you soon. Now, get back to yer paintin'. I expect to be askin' ye for more work soon."

Brynne felt as if she were walking on air as she left the gallery. She was smiling broadly, her eyes were sparkling, and though she tried to control her joy, she couldn't. It was a glorious, wonderful, marvelous day, she decided as she drove out of Kirkcudbright. She couldn't wait to tell Ross.

She drove straight to Fleming House. The butler, who knew her well by now, immediately took her out to the patio, where Ross sat at a table piled high with manuscripts.

"Brynne! You look happy. What happened?"

Brynne bent to kiss him affectionately. "You are looking at an honest-to-God, bona fide *artist*. You can view my work at the Blue Moon Gallery anytime, Monday through Friday, ten o'clock A.M. to six o'clock P.M."

"Congratulations! Why didn't you tell me you were going to see old Farren? I would've gone with you."

"If you'd been with me, Farren might have felt he should be polite to the 'laird's' girlfriend," Brynne said matter-of-factly. "That wasn't what I wanted. I wanted an honest opinion. And if that opinion turned out to be critical, I wanted to be able to slink away and lick my wounds in private."

"You are hopelessly neurotic, like all artists. You're a good painter. And you're getting better all the time. I've been telling you that for weeks."

"Yes, but *you* sleep with me. You have a vested interest in flattering me. Mr. Farren doesn't. His opinion has nothing to do with liking me personally."

"And therefore means more," Ross commented perceptively.

"Only in a financial sense, darling. You give me heartfelt praise and encouragement, he gives me cold hard cash—hopefully," Brynne finished with a sudden spurt of doubt.

"Don't worry. Art lovers will be showering money on you shortly."

"I hope so. I'm doing this to earn a living, you know, not for the dubious pleasure of sitting outside in a rainstorm to capture the right effect on canvas."

Ross looked at her soberly. "Do you need the money so badly, then?"

"Don't worry, I'm not starving," Brynne assured him glibly. "But I've got to start earning a living at some point."

"Because if you *do* need money," Ross persisted, "you know you've only to tell me—"

Before he could quite finish, Brynne interrupted tersely. "No. Thank you, but no. Being a kept woman isn't my style."

"I didn't mean it as payment for services rendered," Ross said curtly, obviously hurt.

"I know that, darling," Brynne hastened to assure him. "And I appreciate the offer. I honestly do. I'm sorry if I sounded like Jane

Eyre refusing Mr. Rochester's generosity. It's just . . ." Brynne paused, searching for the right words to explain to Ross how she felt. She leaned across the table and took his hand in hers.

"You're not responsible for me. I am. I want it that way."

"You're stubborn as hell, you know," Ross replied, but the love in his eyes as he looked at her took the edge off the words.

"So are you. If *I* offered *you* money, would you take it?"

"That's different."

"It's exactly the same. And you know it."

They looked at one another irritably for a moment, each caught up in the righteousness of his position. Suddenly Ross laughed and shook his head. "You're impossible."

Brynne rose and came around the table to him. Sitting down on his lap, she put her arms around his neck and kissed the tip of his nose. "And *you're* wonderful. Instead of spending the weekend fighting, I have a much better idea."

"Do you, now?"

"I do, indeed," Brynne replied, kissing him full on the lips. Ross responded passionately, making desire rise in Brynne as well. Finally Brynne pulled back. Breathlessly she said, "We'll shock the servants."

"To hell with the servants," Ross replied, kissing her again. When they finished, he asked, "What did you have in mind as an alternative to arguing?"

He was smiling and Brynne smiled in return. Now they were both devoid of the anger that had come between them only moments earlier.

"I thought we'd play a game. It's called 'The Barmaid and the Lord of the Manor,'" Brynne teased impishly.

Ross laughed, delighted with her impudence. "Well, before you seduce me entirely, young lady, there's something I want to talk to you about."

"Okay," Brynne agreed, relieved that they were no longer fighting.

"Have you heard of the Edinburgh International Festival?"

"Vaguely. Does it have to do with music?"

"Yes, as well as theater, film, art, dance, just about every art form you can imagine."

"Including bagpipes?" Brynne asked, grinning.

"Yes. Even that incredible instrument. It's the biggest cultural extravaganza in the world. Actually, it's several festivals in one; there's a film festival, a jazz festival, and so on. It's a nonstop celebration for three weeks, starting in late August."

"Sounds wonderful."

"It is. It's a bit crazy, but a great deal of fun. There's a real carnival atmosphere. Performances take place everywhere, even the streets."

"And?" Brynne asked.

"And I'd like you to come to Edinburgh to see the festival with me."

"You mean for a few days?"

"For the entire three weeks. I have a nice apartment there. You'd be very comfortable."

Brynne rose and walked over to the stone wall that ran along the edge of the terrace. Leaning on it, she looked out at the sloping lawn and beyond it to the small lake. After a moment, Ross joined her. Putting his hands on her shoulders, he turned her to face him.

"Brynne, it would give us some time together. Uninterrupted time. This business of seeing each other on weekends just isn't enough."

"But, Ross, it would mean leaving my work just at the point when I'm finally beginning to get somewhere. I'd get nothing done for three weeks."

"You deserve a vacation. Three weeks away from your work won't matter."

Brynne wondered how Ross would react if she said the same thing to him. But she bit back the tart comment. It would only lead to another argument, she knew.

"Brynne, I want to wake up with you, not just for one morning or two mornings, but *every* morning. I want to be with you without the pressure of Monday-morning good-byes."

She couldn't argue with that. She felt exactly the same way. Every Monday when Ross left, she was lonely and miserable. It took hours to get adjusted to life without him. The thought of being with him for a longer time appealed to her far more than she wanted to admit.

Ross continued persuasively, "I want to show you Edinburgh. I want you to meet my friends and see something of my work." He paused, looking at her intently. Then he smiled the familiar heart-turning crooked grin. "Come on, love, it will be fun."

She hesitated. But she couldn't resist him. Seeing Farren earlier had strengthened her resolve to work hard. Now that resolve gave way in the face of Ross's irresistible charm.

"All right. I'll play hooky with you."

"What?" Ross asked, puzzled by the expression.

"It's just a figure of speech," Brynne replied. She didn't explain that it meant turning one's back on work in order to play. But she was painfully aware that she was doing what she had vowed never to do again—putting another person's desires ahead of her own needs.

Chapter Fourteen

*B*rynne was packing for her trip to Edinburgh. Ross was coming by in a few minutes to pick her up, and she didn't want to make him wait. When the phone rang, she answered it absentmindedly, prepared to quickly brush off whoever was calling.

"Miss McAllister, 'tis Sean Farren."

"Mr. Farren! Hello, how are you?" Brynne asked politely.

She hadn't talked to Farren since she'd hung her paintings in his gallery. She knew, as a former gallery owner, that it would be better not to pester him with questions concerning how her paintings were being received. Now she waited breathlessly to hear why he was calling.

"I'm fine, thank you. I called to tell you that both your paintings have been sold. The first sold last weekend. I called to tell you, but you were out. The second sold just a few minutes ago."

Brynne's heart fluttered with relief. Her paintings had sold! She had just earned her first money as an artist. Three hundred pounds, minus Farren's commission, wasn't a great deal. But it was a start. And Brynne was confident she would soon be making more.

"I'll need more of your work," Farren went on. "How soon could you bring something by?"

Brynne thought rapidly. She had three paintings ready to be framed. She and Ross could drop them off on their way out of Kirkcudbright.

"I can be by in about half an hour," Brynne told Farren.

"Good. I'll see you then. Good-bye."

When she hung up, Brynne raced up to the third floor to her gallery, where the paintings were stacked against each other in a corner. Hurriedly she packed them and took them down to her bedroom.

I'm on my way, she thought ecstatically. Then she remembered her plans with Ross—three weeks in Edinburgh. I'll just have to take along my sketchpad and see if I can get some work done, she decided firmly. I can't stop working now.

When Ross arrived a few minutes later, Brynne told him about the sale of her paintings. He congratulated her warmly and quickly agreed to stop by Farren's gallery on their way out of town.

For some reason, Brynne felt reluctant to tell him about her plans to do some work while she was in Edinburgh. She suspected it would only lead to another arugment, and she didn't want their stay together to begin on a sour note.

After stopping at the gallery, Brynne and Ross drove on to Edinburgh. In only a few short hours they arrived at the city. They drove through seemingly endless suburbs before arriving at Ross's apartment in what was known as New Town.

She was surprised to find that this apartment was the opposite of Fleming House. It was relatively small, furnished in a determinedly modern style, with glass-topped tables, brown corduroy furniture styled along straight, Spartan lines, and a noticeable lack of antiques. The paintings that covered the stark white walls were modern also, bold slashes of color in shades of brown, burnt orange and gold.

It was sunny and cheerful. A huge window overlooked the perfect Georgian streets and squares of this part of the city.

"You look surprised," Ross commented as he set down their luggage in the living room.

"It just isn't what I expected after Fleming House. But it's nice, it suits you."

Ross smiled. "Fleming House belongs to my mother, not to me. I went there in the past because it was nice to occasionally get out of the city. And then when I met you, I went much more often. But it isn't the kind of place I would feel comfortable living in permanently. It's too big, too old, too self-consciously historical. I'll probably sell it eventually. I want to live in the present, not the distant past."

Cocking her head to one side, Brynne looked at him speculatively. "No wonder you thought I was silly to buy Castle Fraser. I guess that's a big difference between us. I'm fascinated by the past. And despite what you think, I'm not sure we ever entirely escape it."

She was thinking of Laurie Fraser and her Highland lover. But she didn't say so to Ross. He would only have laughed at her mystical fantasies.

Walking up to Brynne, Ross put his arms around her and pulled her close to him. "Well, it isn't the past I'm thinking of now, my lass. It's the present, particularly this long, private day with you."

He kissed her then, softly, gently, but with a hint of the passion that would come. Brynne responded eagerly, and all thoughts of the past were obliterated as her senses were filled by her intense desire for this man. Before she knew what was happening, Ross scooped her up in his arms and carried her into the bedroom. It was only dimly lit, for the heavy drapes were drawn. But it didn't matter. She wasn't interested in looking at the furnishings at this moment anyway.

That night a strong wind came up, but when Brynne awoke it had died down. Ross lay sound asleep next to her, one arm gently lying across her shoulder. She moved his arm carefully, so as not to wake him, then quietly slipped out of bed. Walking over to the window, she parted the drapes and looked out. The apartment was on the sixth floor of the building, taller than most of the buildings around it. So Brynne had a wonderful view of the surrounding area. Mist was lying on the ground, and the air was still and breathless on this hot August morning. But overhead was just the faintest flush in the grayness, revealing that the sun would break through shortly. Brynne saw vague shapes in the mist. As the mist gradually thinned, the shapes became clearer. Etched in gray, the city emerged, spire by spire, tower by tower. Edinburgh's grandeur was incomparable. Beyond the Georgian section of the city, the New Town, Brynne saw innumerable spires beginning to glow in the rising northern sun. And dominating everything, sitting huge and massive on a tall rock, was Edinburgh Castle.

Suddenly Brynne was aware of the movement behind her. Before she could turn her head, Ross was at her side, putting his arms around her bare waist.

"You're up early," he said sleepily, nuzzling her neck affectionately.

Brynne leaned back against him, loving his hard leanness and the feel of his lips on her skin. "Country folk are early risers," she said in a perfect imitation of a Kirkcudbright accent.

"Well, city folk aren't," Ross responded. "We know there are better things to do than get up with the sun."

"Such as?" Brynne asked impishly.

"Such as *this*," Ross replied, carrying her back to the waiting bed.

Two hours later they were sitting in the small dining room off the living room, eating a light breakfast prepared by Brynne.

"I'll try to get out of the office early today," Ross said. "Tonight's the opening of the festival. The Scottish Opera is performing Puccini's *Manon Lescaut*."

"Sounds marvelous."

"I'll show you around the city a bit first, then we'll have an early dinner before the opera. Afterward, I thought we'd go to a party at my friend Tam's house. He and his wife, Kate, are terrific people. You'll like them."

"Sounds like a very long and full day for you," Brynne commented, sipping coffee. "Will it be this way every day during the festival?"

"Yes." Ross smiled. "One bacchanalian revel after another. There's even a thing called the Marathon, an official competition to see who can attend the greatest number of events in a single day. But I don't think I'll compete. Even though it's festival time, I still have work to do."

"So do I. I brought my sketchbook. I thought I'd do some scenes of Edinburgh."

Ross looked at her soberly, his smile gone. "But I thought you were going to take a vacation, enjoy the festival."

"As you said, there's still work to do. Sean Farren said he expects to sell the new paintings I left with him. If he's right, I'd better have some other work ready soon."

Ross relaxed, giving in gracefully. "All right. I suppose it's selfish of me to want to continue with my own work and have you available when it's convenient for me. But try not to work too hard. I want you to enjoy yourself."

He rose and leaned over to kiss her on the tip of her pert nose. "See you this afternoon. By the way, here's a key so you can let yourself in and out, and a map of the city so you won't get lost."

He handed her the items, then kissed her good-bye.

When he had gone, Brynne quickly cleaned up the breakfast dishes, then took a cup of coffee into the living room. She curled up in a corner of the sofa and thoughtfully sipped the hot, dark liquid. She liked being here with Ross—liked it even more than she had anticipated. Sleeping with him, making breakfast for him, planning how to spend their time together, all seemed natural and right. And yet . . .

A niggling doubt tugged at the back of her mind. As much as he encouraged her in her work, he still seemed to feel her work should come second to him.

Thrusting the irritating thought from her mind, she went into the bedroom and took her sketchbook out of her suitcase. Then she dressed casually in jeans and a bronze silk poet's blouse with full, billowy sleeves. She grabbed a matching cashmere sweater in

case it should turn cool in the afternoon, and
left the apartment.

Outside, she stopped to look at the map.
Ross's apartment was only a few blocks from
Princes Street, the main boulevard of
Edinburgh, and the dividing line between Old
and New Towns. After a short walk, Brynne
left behind the quiet residential section and
found herself surrounded by the festival atmosphere in the business district. It was,
indeed, like a carnival in the streets, and
everything was gaily decorated, reflecting the
old Celtic passion for color and life. People
from all over the world brushed past Brynne
as they went from one cultural event to another.

But Brynne wasn't interested in seeing the
well-known greats of the arts, or the feisty
up-and-coming talents. She wanted to see the
city itself, to explore it, and, hopefully, to find
something that would appeal to her as an
artist.

As she turned onto Princes Street, one of
the most elegant, beautiful boulevards in the
world, she was captivated. On one side, sloping downward behind the shops that lined the
street, was the New Town, designed in the
classical manner. On the other side, in a deep
ravine, were sunken gardens. A sweep of
sward and flowerbeds, with roses swaying in
the gentle breeze, led up to the medieval
buildings of Old Town. There, story upon story
of narrow, centuries-old buildings were piled
against each other on a towering ridge.

Ignoring the shops, Brynne went straight
down to the gardens. Soon she found an

empty bench near a bed of flowers. Sitting down, she took her sketchbook out of her large bag and began drawing the glorious multicolored blooms. Her movements were swift, sure, bold, as she caught the essence of their fluid movement. She sat there for a long while, doing sketch after sketch, before finally closing her sketchbook.

Then she set off to explore Old Town. As she walked down cobbled streets, glancing into narrow closes, she felt her spirits rise. This was the sort of ambience she loved, the mellowness of old stone, the almost tangible sense of history.

Then Brynne saw a gray-and-black-striped cat sitting placidly on a steeply winding stone stairway with a black iron railing. He barely glanced at her as she stopped and stared at him for a moment. There was something about the simple scene that captivated Brynne. The composition was stark, the colors muted.

Pulling out her sketchbook, she sat down on the edge of the sidewalk and began drawing, oblivious of the curious stares of the passersby.

When she finished, she smiled up at the supercilious cat and said gaily, "Thanks for being such a cooperative subject."

Glancing at her watch as she put away her sketchbook, she was surprised to see it was nearly three o'clock. Ross would be home soon, she knew. She didn't know where the hours had gone. She hadn't done much, yet she had enjoyed herself immensely.

As she hurried back toward Ross's apartment, she reflected on how much she had improved as an artist. She knew more about what she was trying to do now, she was more sure of herself. She captured scenes more accurately—the flowers, the expression of the cat. It had to do, at least in part, with Ross, she realized. He brought out aspects of her personality that she'd never suspected existed. Because of her feelings for him, she felt more deeply about everything. And that made her a better artist.

As she crossed Princes Street, Brynne told herself that this was what she would do every day while she was in Edinburgh—simply walk around looking for interesting subjects to sketch.

When she let herself into Ross's apartment a half-hour later, she found him sitting in the living room waiting for her.

"Ah, it's about time you returned. Been taking in some of the festival events?"

"No," Brynne answered, kissing him quickly, then plopping down on the sofa beside him. "I've been drawing flowers and cats, one very superior-looking cat, actually."

"What, no shopping? I thought surely you'd get lost in the shops on Princes Street."

"I probably could have if I'd let myself," Brynne said, smiling. "Fortunately for my finances, I got waylaid by things that were free."

"Well, *I've* been shopping," Ross said, leaning behind the sofa to pick up a package. He set it down on the glass-and-chrome coffee table. "I hope you like it," he finished softly.

"Oh, Ross, I'm sure I will," Brynne responded as she tugged at the silver ribbons on the package.

Ross smiled warmly. "You should see yourself. Your face is lit up like a child's at Christmas."

Brynne grinned. "I know. I'm hopeless when it comes to presents. I *love* them. Big or small, it doesn't matter. Oh!" she finished as she pulled the top off the box and saw what was inside.

Gold glistened. White silk shone. Lace lay fragile and gossamer-thin.

Gently taking the gown out of the tissue-lined box, Brynne saw that it was fit for a queen. It was ankle-length, with a high, round neckline, then see-through white lace plunging nearly to the gold silk ribbon that tied around the waist. There were long, tight sleeves of the same lace, and a narrow skirt of silk.

Looking up at Ross, Brynne saw him watching her intently, a worried look creasing his forehead. "Do you like it?" he asked anxiously. "I didn't know if you would. But as soon as I saw it, I knew I wanted to see you in it. You look especially beautiful in white."

"I *love* it! And I'm not even going to say, 'You shouldn't have,' because I'm so very glad you did." She leaned over and kissed him happily.

When she pulled back, he replied huskily, "Well, you could hardly go to the opera in jeans." Then, before she could respond, he finished firmly, "And we'd better get going on our sightseeing or I suspect I'll never drag myself out of this apartment."

A few minutes later, they were driving up to the top of Arthur's Seat, a hill that rose behind the city. At the very top, Ross stopped the car, and they got out. Below them, the city spread out for miles around. He led Brynne to a grassy area, where they sat down.

"That's the Firth of Forth," he said, pointing to a blue patch of water in the distance. "And that's the Castle Rock, of course," he added, pointing to the castle rising clear and strong in the light of the setting sun.

To the south were the Pentlands and the Moorfoots, to the east the Lammermuirs, and to the north the "Kingdom of Fife." Westward, in graduated shades of blue, were mountains, refined by distance, some purple, some mauve—the Highlands.

Brynne couldn't help thinking that Laurie's lover had come riding out of the Highlands to claim her heart with a love that even death couldn't destroy.

"'Tis a magnificent sight," Ross commented, breaking Brynne's pensive thoughts.

"Yes," she agreed wholeheartedly.

It was a magnificent sight, the city with its ancient grandeur and windy views. Brynne could easily understand how it might be called "the Athens of the North."

"I've fallen in love with your city, Ross," Brynne said, gazing out at the awesome sight.

There was a moment's silence; then Ross said huskily, "And with me as well, I hope."

His arm was around her shoulders as they sat there on the grass, and Brynne felt it tighten slightly with nervousness. Looking up into those changeable hazel eyes, Brynne hesitated for a moment. The warm breeze caressed her face.

It's true, she thought. I feel everything that he wants me to feel, both love and desire.

She answered softly, "Yes . . . with you as well."

It was the first time she had said it, the first time either of them had mentioned the word "love." They had skirted the issue, saying everything else—how much they cared about each other, what their relationship meant to them. Both had known from the beginning that this was no passing affair.

Yet that one word—"love"—had been held back, guarded, in the knowledge that once it was spoken, nothing would ever again be quite the same between them.

"I love you, Brynne. I have from the very beginning—the first moment I looked into your eyes on Beltane. That was a magical night. Maybe it's always magic when two people fall in love. I told myself you'd cast a spell over me. If that was true, I hope it's an enchantment that never ends."

And then he said the words that Brynne had been half-expecting all summer: "Marry me, my sweetest lass."

Brynne looked away. But now her eyes didn't see the stunning panoramic view before her.

When she said nothing for a long moment, Ross asked quietly, "Is it Allen?"

"No," Brynne answered quickly. "Allen would have wanted me to love again, to marry. I wish you could have known him, Ross. He was so full of life, so happy, so open to everything life has to offer. He would want all of that for me now."

"Then what's the problem? We love each other. We're good for each other. I'll make you happy, I swear I will."

"I know, Ross. It's just . . ." She hesitated, searching desperately for the right words to explain her feelings. "I could give myself to you, but I'm not sure what I would be giving. I don't know who I am yet. All my life, I've been defined through someone else—as my parent's daughter, my sister's guardian, Allen's wife. I'm trying to define Brynne McAllister now, and I haven't done it yet."

"Brynne, we've been through this before," Ross said impatiently.

"Yes, but you never seem to understand."

"I understand that we have something most people go through their whole lives without finding—a love that is true and good in every way. Your body excites me, your mind challenges me, and your heart touches me. Compared to that, nothing else matters."

"I have to find my own value before I can know what I'm giving you."

"I know what you're giving me—very great happiness."

Brynne sighed, then leaned her head against Ross's chest. His simple cotton shirt felt cool against her cheek. Her mind was in turmoil, as confusion, intense emotion, desire and fear all raged within her.

Then she pulled away and looked intently at Ross. "I'm not denying you, my love. I'm just asking for more time."

Ross hesitated. Finally he said slowly, "I

don't want to pressure you, love. Let's leave it at this—when the festival is over, before you return to Kirkcudbright, you'll give me your answer."

"Thank you, Ross," Brynne said happily, hugging him tightly. "I *do* need time to think. I'm sorry if I seem coy. It isn't that."

"I know. I didn't think it was." He sighed, then continued abruptly, "Now, we'd better be going or we'll miss the opera."

As they walked back to the car, Brynne knew that their private idyll was almost over. They'd had the summer together, a time when their love was kept private between them. But now reality was intruding on their fantasy. It was inevitable, Brynne realized. But she couldn't help wishing that it didn't have to be so, that the sweet days of summer could continue forever.

Chapter Fifteen

That evening, after the opera, Ross and Brynne walked from the opera house to Tam's apartment. On this warm summer night, the castle and other buildings were floodlit, and their grandeur made Brynne catch her breath in awe.

She and Ross walked hand in hand down the Royal Mile, out of Castle Hill into Lawnmarket, past massive St. Giles's Cathedral, and into the ancient Canongate area. They passed old stone courtyards and dim closes where pale lamps hung above flights of stone steps. The city was redolent of history, and Brynne felt she could almost hear the skirl of bagpipes.

Looking down at Brynne, Ross said lovingly, "You were easily the most beautiful woman at the opera tonight."

She was wearing the lovely white gown. Her only jewelry was diamond studs in her ears. Her hair was pulled back into a sleek chignon, and she had used more makeup than usual so that her eyes stood out, tawny and golden.

Smiling shyly, Brynne replied, "Ah, but it wasn't me, it was this dress. It could transform anyone into a raving beauty. Now, you, sir, are the really elegant one tonight."

Ross was wearing a black tuxedo and white frilled shirt. He was one of the few men Brynne had ever seen who actually looked comfortable in a tuxedo. His lean, lithe build was made for it.

Ross smiled at Brynne's compliment. "Let's just say we're both magnificent tonight," he replied, looking down at her.

"Tell me about your friend Tam."

"I've known him just about forever. He moved next door when we were both ten. We've been through everything together—first love, military service, college."

"He's the photographer who worked with you on the book of castles, isn't he?"

"Yes. We always wanted to do a book together. Finally, we did."

"I wish I had a friend like that," Brynne said wistfully. "Oh, I don't mean that I don't have friends. There are a couple of people in Carmel I'm very close to. But when I was growing up, we moved constantly because my father was a career army man. I went to six different high schools. That made it impossible to develop close, long-lasting friendships."

"But you had Jane."

"Yes, she was the one constant in my life. I guess that's why we're so close now. At least, we *were* close," Brynne finished pensively.

"What happened? I've noticed you haven't talked much about her lately."

"It's the usual story, as old as the hills. She fell in love with a married man."

"And you don't approve," Ross commented simply.

"I can't. I'm concerned about her being hurt. And besides, I keep thinking about his wife and children." At Ross's questioning look she explained, "Yes, there are three children."

"That doesn't sound good."

"No. Jane's with him now. He decided to trade in his wife, whom he apparently finds boring, for a newer model."

"Will Jane marry him?"

"I hope not. But it looks like she may."

"Well, you can't do anything about it, you know," Ross said matter-of-factly. "'Tis her life."

"I know. Believe me, I've stopped playing the wise-older-sister role. But it's awfully hard just sitting back and watching the situation and not saying how I feel."

Suddenly Ross stopped and faced Brynne squarely under the glow of a streetlight. "Tell me something. Are you afraid I would do that to you—get bored and leave you for someone else?"

Brynne smiled softly. "No," she replied confidently. "I can't see you doing that."

He took her in his arms, pulling her against

him, and looked deep into her eyes. "I've been looking for you my whole life. Now that I've finally found you, nothing could ever make me leave you."

Brynne's breath caught in her throat, and she felt weak from the force of Ross's love.

Finally Ross let her go. Holding hands once more, they continued walking down the street. But her heart still beat erratically and her mind was in a whirl.

When they arrived at Tam's apartment, it was filled to capacity with a colorful assortment of people. Some were obviously performers, still wearing their stage makeup. Others were young professionals, like Ross. As they made their way through the crowd, suddenly a young man walked up to them, smiling broadly.

He was short, barely as tall as Brynne, with a flaming thatch of red hair and fair, freckled skin. There was something engaging about him, especially his open, guileless look. Brynne realized immediately that this must be Tam.

"We very nearly couldn't get through this crowd," Ross said, speaking loudly to be heard above the din of conversation and laughter.

"I know. I really didn't intend this, but you know how it is—you invite one or two people, and they bring along a friend or two, and before you know it, half of Edinburgh is in your tiny apartment. Come along, we'll find Kate."

They forced their way through the crowd and finally emerged in a small wood-paneled den. A group of five or six people was sitting on chairs and large pillows strewn around the room, talking animatedly.

Going up to a petite young woman with short black hair and immense green eyes, Tam said, "Kate, look who I've found."

"Ross! We were just talking about you."

She rose and kissed Ross warmly on the cheek. Then she turned to Brynne with a broad, welcoming smile. "I'm sure you must be Brynne. I'm Kate Stirling, and in case he forgot to introduce himself, as he usually does, that's my derelict husband, Tam."

"Pleased to meet you both," Brynne replied, accepting Kate's outstretched hand.

Kate introduced Brynne to the other people in the room, all of whom already knew Ross. One woman, Vivien Tait, a gorgeous blonde with a voluptuous figure and ice-blue eyes, eyed Brynne critically as they were introduced.

Ross and Brynne sat down on pillows in a corner and accepted the glasses of white wine that Kate offered.

"We were just talking about that new book of poetry by John McGregor," Kate continued, speaking to Ross. "That was quite a coup, getting him to sign with your publishing house."

"Not really," Ross replied modestly. "He was unhappy with the way his old publisher was treating him. He was ready for a change."

"Don't be so modest," Tam interrupted. "Every major publisher in Europe was trying to bag old McGregor. How'd you persuade him to come to your classy but admittedly small operation?"

Before Ross could answer, Vivien Tait said curtly, "Probably used the famous Fleming charm. 'Tis well-known that Ross can talk almost anyone into almost anything."

Her pale blue eyes were narrowed in dislike, and it was obvious she was trying to insult Ross. But Brynne didn't understand the source of the animosity.

The awkward silence that followed was broken when Kate said cheerfully, "Well, I can see we're running out of grub. I'd best get into the kitchen and whip up something."

"Good idea. The kitchen's the spot for you, my lass," Tam said, grinning. "Glad to see you've finally realized where a woman's place is."

Glaring at him in mock anger, Kate rose and said to Brynne, "Care to come with me? I could use some help. My husband's comments to the contrary, the fact is, I'm not a very good cook."

"I'd love to help," Brynne replied, getting to her feet.

In the kitchen, Kate took out some bread and potted meat and began preparing sandwiches. Brynne helped, cutting the crusts off the bread and dividing the sandwiches into attractive triangles.

"Actually, as you probably guessed, I didn't really need any help," Kate said as she worked quickly and expertly. "But Vivien was being impossible, and I thought it best to explain matters to you quietly."

Suddenly Brynne had a flash of insight. "I take it she used to date Ross."

"Exactly." Kate looked at Brynne thoughtfully. "You're quick. I can see why Ross is so daft about you. It isn't just your looks."

"Well, I don't know about that . . ." Brynne began with a self-deprecating laugh.

"Take it from me, the man's besotted. And Vivien's fit to be tied. She thought at one point he'd marry her, you see. Though she should've known better. He never indicated he was serious about her. She was just one of several women he was dating."

Suddenly realizing that her words might be taken the wrong way, Kate continued quickly, "Damn my tongue, anyway. I don't mean he's a playboy. Far from it. Tam tells me I say too much sometimes, and perhaps he's right."

"That's okay. I understand."

"Anyway, you've nothing to worry about. Tam told me how Ross feels about you. And 'twas obvious the moment you two walked in tonight. He looks at you the way all women wish a man would look at them."

"And how is that?" Brynne couldn't resist asking.

"Like you're made of spun gold," Kate answered. Then she grinned impishly. "If I didn't have a man I'm already crazy about, I'd be jealous. I don't blame Vivien for being such a bitch about the whole thing. She's a sore loser."

Brynne smiled warmly at Kate. She liked her easy, comfortable manner. She said, "Vivien Tait doesn't strike me as the sort of woman who's doomed to sit home moping. With her looks she must have her choice of men."

"Yes—except for Ross. Unfortunately, he's the one she wants. Well, Viv will just have to console herself with someone else. Which she'll waste no time doing, I'm sure."

"Kate, I'm going to be in Edinburgh for the next two or three weeks. I'd like to have lunch with you sometime, if you're free."

"I'd like that too. And I'm free just about every day. I work out of the apartment, doing free-lance editing, so I can take off just about whenever I choose. I'm busy tomorrow, but what about the next day?"

"Sounds good. Why don't you suggest a place, since I still don't know the city very well."

"All right. I'll think about it and try to come up with someplace quaint and charming. I'll call you on Tuesday morning."

"Great."

"Let's take these in there before the natives get restless and start eating the furniture," Kate said, handing Brynne a tray heaped with small sandwiches.

"Kate . . . thanks for explaining things to me. And for making me feel so welcome."

"'Twas all right, Brynne. I can imagine how difficult it is for you being in a strange city, knowing no one but Ross." She cocked her small heart-shaped face to one side and eyed Brynne carefully. "Besides, you're making Ross awfully happy. And anyone who does that is always welcome in this house."

"You like Ross very much."

"He's a good friend. The best, in fact. He helped Tam once when he needed help desperately, an' I'll never forget that."

"If it's not too personal, may I ask what he did?"

"Of course. It's no secret. Though Ross would never mention it himself. He isn't the sort to do a favor and then brag about it or demand gratitude. Three years ago, Tam was injured in a car accident. He was paralyzed and the doctors said he probably wouldn't walk again. He went into a deep depression, simply gave up on himself, on life—on everything. As far as he was concerned, his life was over. As he said, a photographer who was confined to a wheelchair was no photographer. I tried to convince him otherwise, but he wouldn't listen to me."

"Oh, that must have been *awful*," Brynne said with heartfelt sympathy.

"It was. Then one day Ross showed up with some exercise equipment and a physical therapist, all of which he paid for himself. He told Tam, ''Tis time you got out of that damn chair.' Tam shouted at him—oh, terrible things. I'd never heard him talk to Ross, or anyone, that way before. He was takin' out all of his bitterness an' anger on him. But Ross said nary a word in reply. He just forced Tam to start workin' with the therapist. He came every day to give support an' encouragement. In a year, Tam was walkin' again. He still has a slight limp, but 'tis a small price to pay for bein' able to walk."

Thinking back now, Brynne realized that Tam had walked with a limp when he came across the apartment to greet her and Ross earlier. But it was barely noticeable and she hadn't thought anything of it at the time.

"Ross has spoken to me of you and Tam, but he never said anything about that," Brynne said.

"He wouldn't." Smiling, Kate finished, "Come on, let's feed those animals."

They went into the living room, depositing two of the trays on tables, then took a smaller tray into the den. Brynne sat down next to Ross again and immediately noticed that Vivien Tait was gone. She was immensely relieved, for the beautiful blonde had made her feel distinctly uncomfortable.

They talked long into the night. Ross was easily the center of attention, the person who led the conversation. He was clearly someone whose opinion mattered, a very important person in artistic circles. Until then, Brynne hadn't thought much about Ross's work. She was too caught up in pursuing her own career to be terribly curious about Ross's business.

Now, however, it was apparent to her what an important and successful man Ross was. Somehow, it made her feel just a little bit resentful. No one paid a great deal of attention to her, aside from Kate. No one asked what she did. The fact that she was with Ross seemed all the explanation that was necessary. Brynne found herself wondering whether, if Ross had walked in with Indira Gandhi on his arm, anyone would have given the woman a second thought.

She told herself it was unfair to feel resentful toward Ross, who had done nothing to deserve her anger. Yet she couldn't get over it. And the feeling grew worse as the hours passed.

Then the conversation turned to painting, and an argument about the merits of primitive art.

" 'Tis nothing more than childish muck," a half-drunk young man named Jimmy said stubbornly. "My eight-year-old son could do as well."

Speaking up for the first time all evening, Brynne said patiently, "It's a great deal harder and more complicated than it looks. In primitive art, composition is everything. And composition is immensely difficult."

"I don't agree," Jimmy insisted, taking another sip of wine. "There's *nothing* to it, I say."

"Brynne knows what she's talking about," Ross said quietly but firmly. "She's an artist herself."

Jimmy looked at Brynne with a greater interest than he had shown before. "An artist, you say, Ross? What was your last name again? McAllister?"

"Yes."

"Um, don't think I've ever heard of you."

No, Brynne thought unhappily, you haven't heard of me. No one has, beyond a few people in a tiny village.

"Now, Ross," Jimmy continued, "tell us what John McGregor's *really* like. I hear he's a drunk nowadays."

"That's the pot calling the kettle black," Kate said, grinning. Everyone laughed, including Jimmy, who clearly wasn't easily insulted.

Brynne didn't make an attempt to join the conversation again. She was hurt and angry, and the fact that she knew she had absolutely no justification for either feeling didn't change a thing. She was relieved when Ross finally suggested they leave at nearly three in the morning.

Because it was so late, and they were both exhausted, Ross called a taxi. It carried them through the dark, deserted streets and back to Ross's apartment in a matter of minutes. When they fell into bed, Ross put an arm protectively over Brynne's narrow waist and immediately fell asleep. Though Brynne was equally tired, her mind was racing and she remained awake a long time.

This is what marriage to Ross would be like, she told herself soberly. I'd always be in his shadow. Just like with Allen.

Shadows . . . Brynne finally fell asleep just before dawn, thinking about that word, wondering why there always seemed to be shadows hanging over her life . . . shadows of the past.

Chapter Sixteen

*B*rynne met Kate Stirling on Tuesday at noon in a small pub in Old Town.

"It isn't fancy, but the food's delicious," Kate said as they sat down opposite each other in a wooden booth. "And it absolutely *reeks* of atmosphere. It's been around for centuries."

Brynne smiled and assured Kate that she liked the choice of restaurant. "Ross tends to take me out to expensive restaurants featuring rich continental cuisine. It's nice, for a change, to eat in a place where I can feel comfortable."

"He's just trying to impress you. Wait till after you're married. Then it will be, 'What are you making for dinner?' instead of 'Where would you like to eat?'" Kate replied, grinning.

Brynne hesitated. She didn't know Kate

well enough to speak frankly to her. Yet something about the woman's open, friendly manner made Brynne want to open up to her. Finally she said hesitantly, "We're not engaged, you know."

"Oh? But I thought . . ." Kate stopped, confused. Then she continued, "I assumed it was all set. Ross isn't usually one to let grass grow under his feet, as they say."

"We've talked about marriage," Brynne admitted, "but nothing's settled."

"So that's the way of it," Kate replied thoughtfully.

A plump middle-aged waitress arrived to take their order then. Kate recommended the lamb stew, and when she and Brynne had ordered it, the waitress left.

"'Tis none of my business, of course, but as Tam says, I tend to forge ahead where angels fear to tread," Kate said frankly. "So if you don't mind my askin', what's the problem?"

Brynne smiled gently. "I don't mind."

"It isn't Vivien Tait, I hope. Because she's definitely ancient history, you know."

"I know. Maybe I'm terribly conceited, but I'm not worried about other women. I think I can trust Ross."

"You can indeed. And that's not something I would say about many men. You know, before I married Tam, I dated a lot. And every single man I went out with was the sort I knew I couldn't trust. Then I met Tam, and he was different. When he asked me to marry him, he told me he would never be unfaithful. I knew he meant it. So I married him. That was eight years ago, and I've never regretted it."

"You're lucky."

"Don't I know it! Well, then," Kate went on, propping her elbows on the table and locking her fingers under her chin. "If it isn't other women you're concerned about, what's the problem?"

"I know what marriage to Ross would mean," Brynne answered bluntly. "I would be seen as nothing more than his 'little wife.' I've been through that once, and I'm not willing to go through it again. I've discovered lately that I have a healthy ego that isn't prepared to play second fiddle to anyone."

"Ah, so that's it. 'Tis ironic, you know. Most women would like nothing better than to hang on Ross's arm, to bask in his reflected glory. But you need your own glory."

"Yes. Do you understand?"

"Of course. I've never been overly ambitious, myself. I do a little editing because I enjoy it and it keeps my mind from turning to mush. But all I've ever wanted, really, was a man I could like and respect, a comfortable home, and work that isn't so demanding that it affects my personal life. I'm content to let Tam have the sparkling career. I'm happy with things as they are."

"As I said, you're lucky. Being at peace with yourself is the most important thing in life."

"Yes. But you'll never be content until you've gone as far as your talent will take you," Kate observed perceptively. "You're as ambitious as Ross, which is saying a great deal."

"Yes, and that's the problem. Ross doesn't seem to understand."

"Of course not, poor dear. He's offering you his heart, which, as far as he's concerned, is tantamount to offering you the world. He can't imagine why you should want anything more."

"I envy you, Kate," Brynne admitted, sighing heavily.

"Because my life is peaceful, without conflict? But I pay a price for it, you know. I don't suffer the agonies of conflict that you do, 'tis true. But I'll never savor the sweet taste of success as you will."

"I'm not so sure I'll ever be a success. I'm just another struggling artist. We're a dime a dozen."

"I haven't seen your work, though I'd love to. But I suspect you must be awfully good. Or you wouldn't value your work as much as you do your relationship with Ross."

"That's the problem, isn't it? In some ways, I feel I have to choose between the two, between the freedom to explore my talent fully, and making a commitment to Ross. If I decide in favor of Ross before I'm really established as an artist, and something should happen to him . . . I wouldn't know who or what I was."

"But, Brynne, nothing will happen to Ross."

"You can't say that with absolute certainty. My husband, Allen, was young and healthy. He left me one morning to go jogging. The last thing he said to me was, 'How about muffins for breakfast?' A half-hour later, he was dead from an aneurysm." Brynne finished soberly, "So you see, I've reason to understand how fragile life can be."

"But you can't worry about random chance, Brynne. There's an element of risk in any relationship. But some people are definitely worth it."

Just then the waitress returned with two plates of delicious-looking stew.

"Mm, looks marvelous," Brynne said.

"It is. Enjoy it. Enjoy everything right now. And try not to worry too much. Ross isn't a Neanderthal, you know. He loves you for who you are, and your painting is a part of that. I can't see him making you drop your career to redecorate his flat. If he'd wanted that sort of woman, he'd have married Vivien Tait. She looks decorative on his arm and is a great little homemaker."

Brynne smiled. "Thanks, Kate."

"You and Ross have something special, a love that doesn't happen to everyone. I'm sure you can overcome whatever problems you face."

But as Brynne ate, she couldn't help feeling that Kate, who was so happy with her own life, was being too optimistic about Brynne's.

The following two weeks were hectic, every day jam-packed with things to do. Brynne tried to finish at least one sketch each day for a series of black-and-white paintings she hoped to produce when she returned to Kirkcudbright. Evenings and weekends were filled with festival events. She and Ross went to colorful gatherings where artists and musicians were feted. Scots in plaid evening kilts mingled with formally dressed guests to the strains of traditional bagpipes.

They heard symphonies performed by some of the world's greatest orchestras, including the London Symphony Orchestra and the Scottish National Orchestra. There were mime, modern dance, musicals, poets reading their works, new films from around the world. And finally, there was the traditional Highland offering, the Edinburgh Military Tattoo, a military spectacle dating from over a century earlier.

As Brynne sat next to Ross on bleacher seats on the Castle Esplanade, she saw various regiments march and dance. The Highland dancing, marching and drill displays were a magnificent spectacle, especially at night, under bright floodlights. Brynne felt her blood stir as she watched the kilt-clad figures and heard the melancholy sounds of bagpipes.

"You look enthralled by this," Ross commented when he caught Brynne's rapt expression.

"I was just thinking—it must have been something like this when Laurie's lover, the Lord of the Isles, went off to battle. He would've worn a kilt, and there would have been bagpipes playing the troops into battle."

Ross shook his head in exasperation. "You're hopeless, you know."

"And you have no romance in your soul, Ross Fleming," Brynne said tartly.

"Ah, but you know that isn't true," he responded. Though he kept his voice low so that the crowd around them wouldn't hear, his eyes were alight with love.

Seeing so much love in his eyes, Brynne

forgot her irritation and found herself feeling only profound tenderness toward him. It didn't matter whether he believed in Laurie Fraser's tragic love. All that mattered was the very real love he felt for her.

By the time the festival was nearly over, Brynne was exhausted, tired of Edinburgh and anxious to return to Castle Fraser. She wanted to focus her energies on her own work again. And, more important, she wanted to regain her sense of her own identity. Being with Ross in his social circle made her feel insignificant. Wherever they went, it was Ross to whom people spoke, Ross whose opinion was sought. It reached the point where Brynne began to doubt herself, to wonder who she was.

Perhaps, she thought soberly, I'm nothing more than the latest girl on Ross Fleming's arm.

One morning while Ross still slept, Brynne rose very early. She went into the kitchen and made coffee, then took a cup into the living room. Curling up on the sofa, she read the newspaper, then glanced through the sketches she'd made while in Edinburgh. But she felt restless. And she knew that she needed to talk to someone who was interested in her alone, without Ross. Finally she called Sean Farren to find out how her new paintings were being received at the gallery.

"Brynne! 'Tis about time ye called," he said excitedly. "I've been tryin' to get ahold of you for a week, lass. Your paintings have all sold, an' I want more. 'Tis time to raise the price, too. How does £300 for the smaller ones, an' £400 for the larger ones sound?"

"Oh, Sean, you've no idea how good it sounds. My ego needed a boost."

"You artists are all alike, concerned with yer blasted egos. Let's get down to business—how soon can ye gi' me some more pictures?"

Brynne laughed. "Gallery owners are all the same, too," she said knowingly. "Concerned only with making money."

"Stick to the point. Have ye been workin' or muckin' about at that silly festival?"

"I've been working, for your information. How does a series of black-and-white etchings on Edinburgh sound?"

"Marvelous! If they're good enough, we'll ha' prints made, numbered an' signed by Miss Brynne McAllister hersel'."

"Oh, Sean, do you mean it?"

"O' course. When it comes to money, lass, I'm always serious. So get yer lovely self back to Kirkcudbright an' start makin' both o' us filthy rich."

When Brynne hung up, her mind was racing with plans and schedules. If she took the next train back, she could have enough etchings done to show Sean in a week. In a month, the entire series could be done and the prints made.

"What are you looking so excited about?"

Brynne looked up to see Ross standing in the doorway to the bedroom. He was still in his brown velour robe, and he was rubbing the sleep from his eyes.

Smiling happily, she explained what had happened.

"Wait a minute," he interrupted as she went on about the financial profit that was possible if the prints sold. "What you're saying is you want to go back this morning. But the festival's got three days to go."

"I know, Ross, but I'm anxious to get back to work. There's so much to do. And, frankly, if I see one more concert or play, I think I'll scream. I'd much rather be back at my easel."

Ross sat down beside her on the sofa and put his arm around her. Pulling her against him, he kissed the top of her head affectionately.

"I see. I wish I could argue with you, but I can't. I *do* understand how you feel. And I'm glad your paintings are doing well."

"*But* . . ." Brynne finished for him.

"*But* I don't want you to leave," he admitted with a rueful grin. "I'm selfish enough to want you to stay here with me. These past few weeks have been wonderful, and I don't want them to end."

"Ross, I'm not going to the end of the earth, just to Kirkcudbright."

"Yes, but I can't get down there just now. In fact, I should stay in Edinburgh for the next couple of weeks and get caught up on all the work that's stacked up during the festival."

Looking up at him, Brynne grinned slyly. "Well, if we have to spend some time apart, I can guarantee you I'll make it up to you when we *do* get together again."

"Ah, will you, now?"

"I will indeed," Brynne replied, running her finger along his jawline and down his neck to his chest, where the open robe revealed a mat of soft golden hair.

"When are you leaving?"

"Noon. There's a train then for Kirkcud-bright."

"Do you have to go so soon?"

"Yes. I'm afraid I really do, love."

"Then there's something we must talk about before you go."

"Oh?"

"Impossible woman!" Ross exclaimed in mock anger. "Do you get so many proposals of marriage that you've forgotten mine? If you'll recall, you said you'd give me your answer before you left Edinburgh."

Brynne was silent for a long moment. She looked away, unable to meet Ross's wondering gaze. His attitude had been lightly teasing but confident. Now, however, as Brynne's silence stretched on, he began to frown and his pale eyes narrowed in concern.

"Brynne, I assumed . . . Things have gone so well . . ." He faltered and stopped.

"Yes, but there have been problems."

"I wasn't aware of any."

"No. That's because things are perfect for you. You're in your element here, doing work you love, respected by everyone. You know who you are and where you're going. I'm nothing more than an appendage, decorative but distinctly unimportant."

Without realizing it, her voice had risen in irritation.

When she stopped, Ross replied angrily, "I've never made you feel unimportant!"

"No, but everyone else has. Ross, I make myself feel unimportant. Who am I, after all, but just another person who calls herself a painter?"

"This is ridiculous. You're wallowing in self-pity and using it as an excuse to avoid commitment."

Brynne hesitated, stung by the truth of his accusation. Is that at the heart of it? she wondered. Am I just afraid to commit myself to him?

With an effort, Ross brought his anger under control.

"I'm sorry, lass. I didn't mean to start an argument. What a romantic way to persuade you to marry me," he finished dryly.

Brynne smiled softly, grateful for the olive branch Ross was extending. "Don't apologize. I *do* realize I'm being unfair to you. I said I would give you an answer, and now I'm hedging."

"I know you love me," Ross said softly, but with an undertone of firm conviction. "And 'tis obvious to the whole world that I love you."

"Oh, if only that were all that mattered . . ." Brynne ended on a wistful note.

She felt more torn than she'd ever felt in her life. She was terrified that she would lose Ross, and yet she badly needed this time on her own.

"I can understand how difficult it's been for you," Ross finally said. "Perhaps once you get back to work and feel more sure of yourself . . ." His voice trailed off, and he left the unspoken thought hanging.

"Yes, let's talk again in Kirkcudbright," Brynne replied quickly, anxious to end the argument.

"We'll do a great many things in Kirkcudbright," Ross whispered, nuzzling her cheek. Gently pushing her down on the sofa, he untied her robe and drew it aside to reveal her nakedness. Cupping her breasts in his hands, he moved on top of her and kissed her lightly, quickly, on her face and neck, lingering over the full round breasts.

Brynne relaxed, giving herself fully to the delicious agony of his teasing caresses. At that moment nothing mattered but the sweet ecstasy that only he could give her.

Chapter Seventeen

Summer drifted into fall. The leaves on the trees turned orange, crimson and yellow. The smell of autumn, a warm earthiness, was in the air. And the heather bloomed deep purple; bending back before the cold wind until the smooth smoke-gray stems shone brightly.

It was cold now, even on the sunniest days, and Brynne dressed in warm tweeds, like a true native of Kirkcudbright.

She worked constantly, driving herself as she had never done before. She was filled with an urge to create that obliterated everything else.

Ross came down every weekend. As she had hoped, he was giving her the time she needed. Sometimes, as he lay sleeping beside her, she felt a rush of both love and gratitude toward him.

I want you, Ross Fleming, she thought. I really do. Please give me this time, this gift of understanding. Even though it seems a capricious request.

Then one day she picked up her mail at the Kirkcudbright post office. She found an invitation waiting for her. It was handwritten on thick ivory-colored stationery, in a gently flowing hand. It was from Lady Grace Fleming, Ross's mother, asking if Brynne could join her for tea the next afternoon. Though Brynne wondered what had prompted the invitation, she called Fleming House immediately to accept.

The next day, precisely at four o'clock, the hour mentioned in the invitation, Brynne arrived at Fleming House. She had dressed carefully in a wool suit of lavender tweed, with a matching cashmere sweater that she had bought in Edinburgh. She was anxious to impress Ross's mother, to dispel the image she might have of Brynne as the stereotypical sloppy bohemian artist.

When the butler showed Brynne into the sitting room, where a fire crackled warmly on this crisp October afternoon, Brynne felt her heart flutter nervously.

The middle-aged woman sitting placidly on the sofa near the fire was hardly the sort to inspire fear and trembling. Tiny, barely five feet tall, and inclined to plumpness, she had quintessentially English good looks. Her peaches-and-cream complexion needed only the slightest cosmetic help to look perfect. Her periwinkle-blue eyes sparkled brightly, and her hair, which was expertly styled in short, loose curls framing her face, was the color of expensive champagne.

She was dressed in a stylish knit suit that perfectly matched the color of her eyes. Her only jewelry was a string of pearls that shone softly against the blue background. Everything about her—her regal carriage, her clothes, her surroundings in the exquisitely furnished sitting room—indicated wealth and breeding. Yet instead of being intimidating, her smile was warmly welcoming and her eyes were kind.

"Brynne, I'm so glad you could come on such short notice. Do sit down here," she invited, patting the sofa beside her. "I hope you don't mind my calling you Brynne. 'Miss McAllister' seems so formal. And nowadays one can thankfully dispense with those old-fashioned formalities. I always thought it was a bit stilted calling everyone but your family by his last name."

She chattered on easily, with disarming candor, and Brynne wondered why on earth she had ever felt nervous about this meeting.

"I'm glad you invited me," Brynne replied when Lady Grace finally gave her a chance to speak. "I've heard so much about you from Ross."

"And I, of course, have heard a great deal about you from my son," Lady Grace responded. "Actually, I've been wanting to get up here for some time, but things kept happening. I made the mistake of going on one of those round-the-world cruises. Quite restful, actually, but after a few weeks, every port began to look the same. I was glad to get back to London, to my garden and my friends." Suddenly shifting topics practically in mid-sentence, she finished, "I must say, you're not at *all* what I expected."

"Oh?" Brynne managed to ask, wondering if this were a compliment or an insult.

"You're everything Ross said, of course, pretty and obviously quite nice. But considering how hard you're being on the poor boy, I expected someone a bit more gimlet-eyed."

Brynne laughed in spite of herself, and Lady Grace smiled broadly. She went on candidly, "No, you're not at all hard. That's why I can't understand it."

"I'm not sure I follow you," Brynne responded hesitantly.

"I'm probably being vague, as usual. *I* always know what I mean, but other people seem to have a hard time understanding me. You see, my son's had girls running after him since he was fourteen. It never occurred to me that when he finally decided to settle down, the girl might reject him. He tells me you refuse to marry him. Though I'm admittedly prejudiced, I think it's fair to say he's rather good-looking. And financially he's very well set. So I find your stubbornness intriguing. You're not a Bolshevist, are you, one of those people who are inherently opposed to wealth?"

"No," Brynne answered, smiling. "I quite enjoy the things money can buy. Given a choice, I would definitely prefer not to be poor."

"Oh, good. So often I find that artists and writers feel guilty if they're not starving in a garret. So silly, really, because how can you do your best work on an empty stomach?"

Brynne couldn't help laughing. Lady Grace was a joy, rather dithery but definitely a dear. Brynne understood now why Ross was so fond of his mother. But there was something she had to say, and she decided it would be best to simply come right out with it.

"Forgive me for speaking bluntly, but I'm sure I'm not your vision of the ideal daughter-in-law. I've been married before and I'm hardly on Ross's social level."

"And you think that matters? I should have thought Ross would've disabused you of that notion right off. Any woman who will love my son in the way he needs to be loved is acceptable to me."

She watched Brynne shrewdly, her blue eyes sparkling. "So, tell me, young lady, why don't you want to marry my son?"

"I . . ." Brynne hesitated. Lady Grace was a daunting individual behind that soft facade. Finally she said, "Why does it always have to lead to marriage, anyway? Why can't we just go on as we are? Most men would be happy not to be pressured into making a commitment."

"Ross isn't most men. And you, clearly, are *not* most women. Perhaps you don't really love Ross," she finished speculatively.

Without thinking, Brynne said softly, "I love him far too much."

Lady Grace smiled. "Well, that's a relief. So

long as you feel that way, whatever's wrong can be mended. I'm glad to hear you admit it, at any rate. For a moment I was afraid you'd be too proud."

"What does pride have to do with it?"

"Obviously it's your pride that's the stumbling block. You're afraid you'll have to sacrifice it on the altar of matrimony, so to speak."

"It's not pride," Brynne insisted. "At least not in the sense of being too proud. I simply want to explore myself, my talent. What I want is the right, and the time, to be the most I can be. I'm ambitious, not necessarily for money, although I'm practical enough about money. I'm ambitious for achievement, on my own, without Ross's influence."

"You're as subborn and independent as my son," Lady Grace commented, smiling gently.

Brynne admitted reluctantly, "I love Ross so much that I have to fight a constant battle not to give in to him completely. He could dominate me quite easily if he ever chose to try."

"Has he ever used your feeling for him against you?"

"No."

"And he never will. That isn't his way. He values pride too much to ever want to bend yours to his will."

At that moment there was a soft knock at the door, and a moment later the butler entered with the tea tray. Brynne had seen the exquisite silver tea service many times before, but she never ceased to be impressed by it. Its gently flowing lines were utterly perfect. Lady Grace poured out two cups of tea, then asked Brynne if she would like sugar or milk.

"Neither, thank you," Brynne responded, accepting the cup that Lady Grace offered her.

"I see Cook's made those delicious raspberry scones," Lady Grace went on happily. "And those delightful little shrimp sandwiches. Please have some, my dear."

"Thank you." Brynne put one of the open-faced sandwiches on her plate, then took a bite. It was delicious.

Lady Grace bit into a scone and commented, "The nice thing about the country is that one can eat even more than usual and tell oneself the fresh country air is responsible for the increased appetite."

Brynne smiled with her. She liked Lady Grace and was enjoying this meeting much more than she had expected to.

After taking a sip of tea, Lady Grace said more seriously, "I think I should explain something to you about Ross. His father was a charming man, the sort my mother would have said could 'charm your bloomers off.' But he wasn't the sort to be faithful. He was, in short, an incurable philanderer."

Lady Grace was no longer smiling now, and Brynne realized that this was a painful subject for her.

She went on quietly, "Because of that, there was a great deal of tension in our home when Ross was growing up. He saw what was happening, of course. I'm afraid I couldn't always keep up a bold front about it. He was especially sensitive to the times when my pride was injured by my husband's behavior."

She paused to take another sip of tea; to collect herself, Brynne realized. Then she continued, "I think that experience made Ross especially sensitive to the importance of maintaining dignity. He's always been careful never to take away anyone's dignity, even when he's dealing with people he dislikes. So you see, my dear, you need never fear that Ross would want marriage as a means of keeping you under his thumb."

"But *why* does it always have to be marriage?" Brynne asked passionately.

"Do you really want to be completely free, child? You'll find that absolute freedom is terribly lonely."

"You don't understand."

"How typical of youth. You assume that because I'm a great deal older than you, I've never shared your feelings or experiences. Which is rubbish, of course, because there's nothing new, you know. Everything that's happened now has happened before, to others. Believe it or not, Brynne, I understand all too well how you feel. And I even sympathize with you."

"You do?"

"Yes, but don't tell Ross. He thinks I should be completely on his side. I understand that it's a mistake to take someone's freedom away before he's ready to relinquish it. When I met Ross's father, it was toward the end of World War II. It was an exciting, dangerous, romantic time. I fell head over heels in love with him at first sight."

Even now, Lady Grace's eyes lit up at the thought of her late husband, and Brynne realized that she must have loved him very deeply indeed.

"He was a fighter pilot in the Royal Air Force. Cut quite a dashing figure, I can tell you. He didn't want to get married, but I did. Oh, I did most dreadfully. He kept telling me he wasn't the type to settle down, but I refused to believe him. I was convinced that I could make him happy, could make him stop longing for his freedom. Well," Lady Grace went on quietly, "I was wrong. I persuaded him to do something he wasn't ready to do. And we both lived to regret it. He couldn't give me the commitment I wanted, and I couldn't let him be free as he wished."

Sighing, she finished soberly, "So you see, child, I *do* understand how you feel. And I believe Ross must let you make up your own mind without pressuring you. I only hope that you will think about what your pride is costing you."

Brynne left then and went back to the castle. She tried to put Lady Grace's unsettling words out of her mind as she worked on her paintings. But the words lingered at the back of her mind. Lady Grace's accusation that she was too proud and independent to love had a familiar ring to it. Finally she realized where she'd heard it before. Donald had told her that Laurie Fraser was too proud to give herself to her lover, until it was too late.

Chapter Eighteen

Ross walked into the drawing room, where his mother was having a midmorning cup of tea. Lady Grace looked up and smiled warmly.

"Ross, dear, you must have driven that car at an indecent speed to get here so early."

Ross bent to kiss his mother's cheek, then sat down opposite her. "I assure you, I practically crawled the entire distance."

"I don't believe it, but I'm still glad to see you."

"That cruise did you a world of good, Mother. You're looking marvelous."

"Thank you, dear. But before we get off on boring talk about that endless cruise, I must tell you I've met your young lady. She came to tea yesterday."

"Brynne?" Ross asked, startled.

"Yes, Brynne—unless you've more than one young lady at the moment."

Ignoring his mother's teasing, Ross asked quickly, "What did you think?"

"Not at all what I expected. Much more vulnerable, somehow."

"Vulnerable?"

"Yes. And terribly independent. Of course, that's the problem between you two, isn't it?"

"Yes, and I don't understand it. I'm not asking her to give up anything."

"No, I don't imagine you would understand it. You've had the advantage of wealth and position. You've never doubted your place in the world."

"Mother, you're being vague as usual. I don't see what that has to do with the fact that I can't seem to persuade the girl to marry me and let me make an honest woman of her."

"That's because you're looking at it from *your* point of view and not hers. She sees you—successful, socially prominent, with a title, whether you choose to use it or not. And she thinks she doesn't measure up."

"That's ridiculous!" Ross exploded.

"To you, perhaps, but not to her. She's not the sort who wants to fulfill herself through her husband. Which does her credit, I think. She wants to come to you as your equal. Any other way is just too threatening to her."

"I don't see how I'm a threat to her."

"That's because you're thinking only of what you want, and not what she needs. You want her and you refuse to understand why you may not be able to have her. It's my fault, I suppose. I spoiled you dreadfully."

Ross smiled indulgently at his mother. "Yes, you did. But I don't think I'm being unfair to Brynne. I'm not asking her to give up her career. I'm very supportive of it, in fact."

"Yes, but you're asking her to give up her freedom. And until she can do that without feeling she's giving up all control, she'll continue to be obstinate."

"Well, I'm *not* going to let this drag on much longer. I intend to marry her and make her happy, in spite of herself."

"Ross . . . don't force her. She loves you most dreadfully, and if you insist, you probably could force her into marrying you now. But she isn't ready. She's got to come to you willingly or not at all. Give her the freedom she needs right now. The more freedom you give a person, the more you can then have of that person. It's like a handful of sand. The tighter you squeeze, the more you lose."

Ross was thoughtful for a moment. Then he said slowly, "I'm thirty-five years old. I've found the woman I want to spend the rest of my life with, and I want to get on with it. I want to have children while I'm still young enough to play with them."

"And what about Brynne? Does she even want children?"

"Of course she does. She'll be a wonderful mother."

"Perhaps. But you haven't even asked her about that, have you? Really, Ross, you must stop playing the domineering male and start giving some thought to Brynne's feelings."

"Whose side are you on, anyway?" Ross asked with a wry smile.

"Yours, dear. Always. But if you want your heart's desire, you're going about it the wrong way."

"I think Brynne simply needs some help in making up her mind."

Lady Grace sighed exasperatedly. "Really, Ross, you're impossible. I wonder that the girl loves you at all."

"Well, she does. And I love her. And that's all that matters. Everything else is just talk. I'll give her more time, but not a great deal."

He rose. "And speaking of Brynne, I'm going to run over and see her now. How would you feel if I invited her to dinner tonight?"

"That's fine, of course. I'll tell Cook to prepare something special."

As Ross turned to leave, Lady Grace said pointedly, "Remember what I said about the sand, Ross."

"I will," Ross replied agreeably. But as he went out, his mind was on a Christmas wedding.

Brynne sat on the sofa in her living room, reading the letter from Jane for the second time. She was stunned but excited. Jane had written:

> I showed Jason the painting you sent, the one of the heather in the rain. He wants to see some more. He loves it! He asked if I thought you'd be interested in exhibiting in the gallery. I said, "Maybe," not wanting to sound too eager,

and told him you'd call to discuss it. Brynne, isn't this marvelous? Call him immediately, then call me and let me know what's happening. By the way, you owe me a commission as your agent! But you can forget it, if you'll just come back for a visit.

> Love,
> Jane

Brynne had never felt such excitement and nervousness at the same time. To be exhibited in Carmel could make her reputation as an artist. And yet . . . that was where Allen had known such success. To have her work shown in the same gallery where his had been shown would invite comparisons that Brynne wasn't sure she was ready to handle.

Well, I can't run away from that forever, she told herself pragmatically. At some point I've got to expand beyond Kirkcudbright. And this is an opportunity that is too good to miss.

She called Jason that night when it was still morning in Carmel.

"Brynne, love, how wonderful to hear your voice! I think I detect a bit of a Scots accent."

Brynne laughed. "Well, *you* haven't changed, Jason."

"Brynne, I must tell you how impressed I was with that painting Jane showed me. Frankly, I couldn't believe it was yours. It was so different from the things you did here."

"I've changed my style," Brynne said succinctly.

"I should say so. I'd love to see more of your work. Are you being shown anywhere?"

"Just in a local gallery in Kirkcudbright."

"Can you send me two or three paintings?"

"Of course. Right away."

"After I've seen them, we'll talk again."

Brynne realized he was suggesting that if he liked her work enough, he would be willing to have a show for her. But until he saw more of her work, he wouldn't commit himself.

"I'll ship some things tomorrow, Jason."

"Good. Now, enough talk about work. Tell me how you like Scotland."

"I love it. It's been very good for me."

"So Jane says. She also says you've found yourself one hell of a sexy Scot."

Brynne laughed. Trust Jason to know everything. "Yes," she admitted, "he is very sexy. But not nearly as charming as you, Jason," she added teasingly.

Jason laughed appreciatively. "Of course. No one has my charm." Then he finished, his tone more serious, "I'm glad you're making such a marvelous new life for yourself, Brynne. It's what Allen would have wanted for you."

"I know," Brynne replied softly. She realized that Jason was giving her his blessing regarding Ross, and she appreciated that. Jason had known Allen well, and liked him immensely. It would be understandable if Jason was reluctant to see her involved with another man only a year after Allen's death.

Then, remembering his gift of the silver scissors, Brynne realized Jason wasn't that way. His philosophy was that the past should be put behind one; life was meant to be lived.

It was not unlike Ross's philosophy of living, Brynne realized.

"Brynne, love, I must go," Jason finished. "I have an appointment with a client who has no taste but a great deal of money."

"Take care, Jason. I hope I see you soon."

"I'm sure you will, love. 'Bye."

When she hung up, Brynne was grinning from ear to ear. She was only one step away from having her own show in Carmel. And while that thought was frightening, it was also very, very exciting.

Chapter Nineteen

October 29 was Brynne's birthday. It was a Friday and Ross came down early from Edinburgh to be with her. They had dinner at a small restaurant in Kirkcudbright, then returned early to the castle. As they walked into the living room, Brynne said, "There's wine in the refrigerator. Why don't you open it while I slip into something more comfortable?"

"Mm, sounds good," Ross replied, kissing her quickly on the cheek before heading into the kitchen.

In her bedroom, Brynne took off the burgundy cashmere wraparound dress she'd been wearing and slipped into a white silk caftan. Then she put on flat gold sandals that laced around her ankles.

As she sat down at her vanity table to brush her hair, which she had worn loose and gently waved that evening, she looked at her reflection in the mirror. Her eyes sparkled with tiny points of light. Her pale cheeks were flushed with excitement. Her entire demeanor was that of a woman who is completely fulfilled in every way.

A year ago she had felt lost and confused. Her movements were slow, hesitant, unsure. The center had gone from her life, and she didn't know how to fill the void. Now all of that was changed, and she knew she had Ross to thank. He made her feel glad to be alive, glad to be a woman. He brought joy and passion and meaning to her life.

When she had come to Scotland in search of a romantic adventure, Brynne hadn't dreamed that she would find this . . . this ecstasy.

As she went downstairs, Brynne wished she could find some way to thank Ross for all he'd given her.

He was sitting on the sofa in the living room, pouring the wine into tall crystal goblets. He'd lit the fire in the fireplace and it was beginning to crackle pleasantly. Outside, a light rain was pattering against the windows, but inside, all was warm and cozy.

Brynne sat down in a corner of the sofa, curling her feet beneath her, and accepted the glass of wine that Ross offered.

Holding up his own glass, Ross said, smiling, "A toast is in order, I think. To your first and last thirty-second birthday."

"Oh," Brynne groaned, "don't remind me."

"Now, don't be silly about it. You're practically a child still."

"Then why do I feel positively ancient?" Brynne asked ruefully.

"Because you accept the common illusion that 'tis better to be terribly young. But I'll tell you something, love. Every one of your thirty-two years has helped make you the wise, wonderful, sexy woman you are right now. And I, for one, am glad."

Brynne put her arms around Ross's neck and looked up into his hazel eyes. "What an absolutely lovely thing to say. I could almost grow old happily if you told me that every year."

"I intend to," Ross replied, kissing her gently, teasingly. Pulling away reluctantly, he finished, "Now, before you seduce me, I want to give you something."

From his pocket he pulled out a tiny gold-wrapped package and handed it to Brynne. His expression was just a bit nervous but hopeful.

Brynne knew what it was before she opened it. Still, she was surprised at the size of the blood-red ruby and the diamonds surrounding it. She didn't take it from the velvet-lined box, but simply stared at it for several seconds.

Finally Ross said hesitantly, "I hope you like rubies. I thought it would look nice against your fair skin."

Reaching out, he took the ring from the box, then continued, "And in case you've any doubts, it's meant for *this* finger."

He slipped it on her left hand. Against the

creamy porcelain of Brynne's skin, the ruby glowed wine-dark, and the diamonds sparkled with the clearest, whitest light.

Brynne looked up at Ross, her eyes glistening with tears. "Ross, it's *magnificent*, but—"

"Shh," he said, putting a finger lightly to her lips. "Say no more. I only want to hear that you like it and will accept it. Because my heart goes with it, lass."

"Oh, Ross, of course I accept it."

Before Brynne could continue, the telephone rang. Feeling irritated at the interruption, Brynne rose and walked across the room to the small rosewood desk where the phone sat.

Picking up the receiver, she said, "Hello."

"Brynne, love, it's Jason."

"Oh, Jason, hello."

"Are you all right? You sound a bit shaky. Or is it this damned connection?"

"It must be the connection. I'm fine," Brynne replied, glancing at Ross lovingly.

"Well, I *have* to tell you how much I liked the paintings you sent. So much, in fact, that I want to have a one-woman show."

"Jason, do you mean it?" Brynne asked excitedly.

"Of course I mean it. I showed your pictures to the art critic from the San Francisco *Chronicle*, who happened to be in town, and he was most impressed. He agreed to cover the show. There's just one thing. The only free time I have to do it is in three weeks. Could you get together enough pictures by then?"

"I think so. I have about a dozen finished right now."

"I'll need at least six more. So work your lovely little derriere off and be in Carmel by November 20. We'll do the usual fifty-fifty split."

"The usual is sixty-forty, Jason. *You* get the forty."

Brynne could hear Jason sighing over the line. "Ah, Brynne, living in a castle hasn't made you one bit less of a businesswoman, I see. All right, sixty-forty. Now, get to work, love. And I'll see you in three weeks."

"'Bye, Jason. And thank you."

Brynne hung up and stood by the phone for a moment. It was really happening. Even after she'd spoken to Jason the last time and sent him the pictures, she couldn't quite bring herself to believe that this would actually come to pass. In three weeks she would have a one-woman show at a prestigious Carmel gallery.

She was on her way.

"What is it?" Ross asked.

Brynne walked back to the sofa and sat down next to him. Briefly she explained what Jason was arranging.

"A one-woman show, eh? Sounds impressive. You've really arrived as an artist."

"*If* the public likes my work. If they don't like it, and don't buy it, it will be my first and last one-woman show. And that critic could tear me to pieces."

"The public will love your work. And so will the critic, if he has a brain in his head," Ross assured her. Then he added, "I have a suggestion. Why don't we make the trip to Carmel our honeymoon? We could get married here, then go there together for your show. I can get away from the office for a while."

Brynne looked down at the ring glowing deep red on her finger. The diamonds sparkled brightly around it.

"Ross . . ." She faltered, unsure how to explain to him how she felt. This wasn't the way she wanted things to happen with him. He dominated her life here in Scotland, but Allen's shadow still hung over Carmel. She wanted this show, not to take anything away from Allen, but to close that part of her life, to finish what they had started together. She couldn't honeymoon in Carmel with Ross, because in her heart she still saw that as Allen's place.

"This show is very important to me," she continued hesitantly, trying to find the right words that would make him understand. "Not just in terms of my career, but emotionally. People will be sure to compare me with Allen. I'll have to deal with his memory all over again."

"But I'll be there to help you," Ross insisted.

Brynne realized then that she was going to have to say how she felt bluntly and risk Ross's anger.

"Ross, I can't marry you yet. I've got to see what happens in Carmel first. That will determine so many things, especially how I feel about myself as an artist."

Ross's expression went cold with anger. Forcing himself to sound calm, he said, "Brynne, I realize that when we first met I was wrong in forcing myself on you. At that time, all you wanted to think about was yourself and your work and putting Allen's death behind you. But I had found you when I was beginning to think I would never know real love. And I was so terrified of losing you that I tried immediately to make you mine when you didn't want to belong to anyone but yourself."

He went on, with growing passion, "But now you're getting your life together. Surely you realize that we can be married without either of us sacrificing the things that matter to us. I would never hold you back in any way."

"Ross, please just wait until this show in Carmel is over. Give me this time. When I come back, I'll be yours completely."

"Brynne, you're just using this show as another excuse! When I first asked you to marry me in Edinburgh, you said, 'Wait until the festival is over.' Then you said, 'Wait until I go back to Kirkcudbright.' Now, you're saying, 'Wait until I return from Carmel.' It's just another excuse to run away from making a commitment to me."

"Ross, I can't give myself to you if I don't know who I am. And I won't know that until I find out if I can make it as an artist . . . until I exorcise my feelings of inadequacy regarding Allen."

Ross rose angrily and strode over to the fireplace. He put one hand on the mantel and gazed down into the fire. The rigid set of his shoulders, the tight line of his mouth, revealed how angry he was.

He doesn't understand, Brynne realized with a sinking feeling. At this moment he doesn't even see how much I love him, how desperately I need him.

But she couldn't do as he asked, not yet. She needed to know that she was in charge of her destiny, that shadows of the past weren't going to fall over her new life.

Finally Ross said slowly, "I've been patient, Brynne, but I won't wait forever. I want to make a life with you. And if you don't want the same thing, then be honest about it and stop making excuses."

"Oh, Ross." She rose and went to him, placing her hands on his shoulders. Looking at him intently, she said, "Don't you know what you mean to me? How very much I love you? Until I met you, I didn't really know what love could be."

"Then be mine *now!*" he urged impatiently.

"I *can't*, love. Not yet."

Ross turned and headed toward the door. Stopping at the closet, he took out his coat and put it on.

"There's nothing left to say," he finished tersely. "Good-bye."

He left, slamming the door behind him. After a few seconds Brynne heard the roar of the Porsche's engine as he revved it up and sped away.

Her heart had sunk and her throat was constricted with tears. She didn't know if he was walking out of her life forever. His pride was deeply injured, she knew, and that was one thing he might not ever be able to forgive.

But she couldn't do as he asked, not yet. She could only hope and pray that he would wait for her.

Chapter Twenty

"Brynne!"

Brynne looked in the direction from which the shout came. She saw Jane waving at her from a crowd of people waiting for passengers arriving on the flight from Glasgow to San Francisco. Smiling happily, Brynne hurried over to her.

They hugged warmly. Each was so glad to see the other that the anger from their last, bitter argument at the castle was completely forgotten.

"Let's get your luggage and get out of this madhouse," Jane said, grinning.

"Good idea. After eleven hours on the plane, I'm anxious to be outdoors for a change."

A few minutes later they had collected Brynne's suitcase and tote and deposited them in the trunk of Jane's yellow Volkswagen. Jane expertly negotiated the heavy traffic of San Francisco International Airport, and once out of the city, she turned south on Highway 1. The highway ran beside the ocean, and as Brynne looked out at the pounding surf, she found it hard to believe she was half a world away from Castle Fraser—and Ross.

He hadn't contacted her in the three weeks since their argument. Several times she'd picked up the telephone, wanting badly to call him, to end their disagreement. But she knew they would simply have the same old argument again. Finally she'd decided to wait until she returned from Carmel to contact him. Hopefully by then his anger would be gone.

When they passed Monterey, Jane turned off onto the scenic Seventeen-Mile Drive that led to Carmel. The road skirted Del Monte Forest, which contained thousands of acres of pines, live oak and manzanita, mountain laurel and wild lilac. The forest swept out to the edge of surf-beaten cliffs, along which were scattered lonely little rock islands where seals and cormorants basked in the sun. The air was filled with restlessly wheeling seagulls. The drive wandered among the gaunt cypress trees, their twisted branches straining back from the stormy winds.

Brynne loved this area, with its wind and sun and sea mist. The shadowed paths and dim solitude of the forest were utterly peaceful.

"Want to stop at the lodge for a drink?" Jane asked as they passed the famous Pebble Beach Golf Course.

"Not right now, if you don't mind. I'm anxious to get home and see how everything is."

"Is your house-sitter still there?"

"No, I told her I needed to use the house this week, and she agreed to stay with her family."

"I made reservations at a restaurant on Cannery Row for dinner tonight," Jane said. "If you're not too tired with jet lag."

She and Brynne had eaten often in the area made famous by John Steinbeck. Once warehouses and canneries, the area now featured boutiques and restaurants.

"Sounds great," Brynne replied. "I'll just take a nap first, then I'll meet you there so you don't have to drive all the way back to Carmel again."

They were entering the village now. Brynne was glad to see it after all these months. Its very familiarity was comforting. Yet she didn't feel the pull of home here. Castle Fraser was now her home.

Actually, she thought poignantly, wherever Ross Fleming is, is my home. Because my heart is with him.

When they drove up to Brynne's small cottage, she took her one suitcase and tote out of the car.

"I guess you really don't intend to stay, if that's all the luggage you brought," Jane said ruefully.

"I'm afraid not, Janey. In fact, I'm going to put the house up for sale while I'm here. I didn't tell you over the phone because I wanted to do it in person."

"I understand. It's not exactly a big surprise," she admitted as they entered the house.

Brynne looked around wonderingly. It was all the same. The college student who had been living there had kept it immaculate and had changed nothing, not even the position of the ornaments on the mantelpiece. But Brynne felt no emotional attachment to the place now. It was merely a house where she had once lived, at another time, when she was another person.

Jane went into the kitchen, then shouted through the open door, "Want some tea?"

"Yes," Brynne replied, taking off the plum-colored velvet blazer that she had worn over wool slacks and a striped silk blouse.

While Jane made the tea, Brynne built a fire. And by the time Jane came back into the living room with the tea tray, the fire was beginning to burn nicely, taking the chill off the room.

"Hot tea and a warm fire—what more could anyone want on a cold November day?" Jane said, setting down the tray on the coffee table.

"Jane, it was nice of you to drive all the way to San Francisco to get me. I know you probably had a million other things to do. The holidays are your busiest season."

"Not yet. Most people cook Thanksgiving dinner themselves, then hire caterers to handle the Christmas and New Year's parties."

"What about Todd? Won't he be expecting you?"

Jane hesitated as she stirred sugar into her tea.

Finally she looked up at Brynne. Her dark eyes glistened with barely suppressed tears, but her voice was determinedly firm. "I'm not involved with Todd now."

"Oh." After a moment Brynne continued gently, "I'm so sorry, Janey."

"I know. And it's okay, really. Actually, I'm glad you're here. I want to talk about what happened, and there's no one else who will understand. I don't know," she continued, sighing heavily. "Maybe I'm crazy. Sometimes when I miss him terribly, I think I *must* be crazy to have left him."

"You left him?"

"Yeah. Believe it or not. Last week." Seeing Brynne's puzzled look, Jane explained. "At first, everything was great. We lived in my tiny apartment for a while, but Todd said he was used to a bigger place, so he rented a house at Pebble Beach. It had an ocean view and a maid. I tell you, Brynne, I could get used to that kind of luxury," Jane teased, with a brave attempt at her old humor.

"I can imagine," Brynne agreed, smiling tenderly at her sister.

"Todd filed for legal separation from his wife, and he said when they worked out the property settlement he would get a divorce. For a while I was happier than I've ever been in my life."

"What happened?"

"I ran into his wife. Well, it was bound to happen, I guess. She lives in Pebble Beach too, and it's a tiny community. We just happened to go to the same luncheon."

"That certainly must have been awkward," Brynne said sympathetically.

"It was awful! I've never felt so ill-at-ease in my life. Betty—that's her name—handled it with a lot more class than I did. She introduced herself to me. She said that if I felt awkward about the situation, she would leave because I knew our hostess much better than she did, and it wasn't as important to her to stay."

"She sounds nice."

"Exactly. She *is* nice. And *very* attractive. Even after having three kids, she hasn't let herself go at all. From the way Todd talked about her, I had this image of a slatternly bitch. She wasn't at all what I expected. There I was, standing face to face with the woman I was replacing, and she was someone who could easily have been my friend under other circumstances."

"And you felt guilty," Brynne commented perceptively.

"Yes, but it was more than that. When I first fell in love with Todd, I felt absolutely triumphant. He told me that I made him feel alive again, while with his wife he felt like he was just going through the motions of living. I told myself Todd was blameless. It was Betty's fault the marriage failed."

Shaking her head at her naiveté, Jane continued, "Then when I met Betty and liked her, I found myself sympathizing with her. And instead of seeing her as a rival I had defeated,

I began to see her as someone I might become one day, someone whose fate I might share."

"You mean, if Todd left this nice, pretty woman, he might do the same to you."

"Yes. I'd simply never thought of Todd in that way before. But as I talked to Betty and realized she was a perfectly nice woman who didn't deserve to be abandoned with three young children, it made me feel differently about Todd. After all, what kind of man would do that?"

"Not a very nice one," Brynne said bluntly, relieved that she could finally tell Jane exactly what she thought of Todd.

"No. And not one who could be trusted." Jane's voice trailed off and she was silent for a while.

Looking at her, Brynne saw that her face was drawn in a way it hadn't been before, and her eyes were clouded with unhappiness. She was no longer the carefree, confident young woman she had once been. And Brynne knew that, while Jane would eventually recover, she would never again be quite the same. Jane had always assumed she could have exactly what she wanted from life. Now she had learned that the price for some things is just too high.

Jane continued slowly, "Things weren't the same with Todd after that. I kept thinking about Betty. I couldn't stand what I was doing to her and to her children. And I saw Todd differently. Finally I told Todd it was over and walked out. You know what he did?"

"I can guess. He went back to his wife."

"Yeah." Jane shook her head musingly. "Isn't that funny?"

But her tone was anything but amused.

"You still love him, don't you, Janey?" Brynne asked.

"Yes, *dammit*, I do! It's not so bad during the day, but sometimes at night I cry like a baby."

"Oh, Janey," Brynne said tenderly, and hugged her tightly. "I know it doesn't help, really, but I'm so proud of you. You did the right thing when it was awfully hard to do."

Jane sat back and wiped a tear that had trickled down her cheek. She responded wryly, "You're right—it doesn't help. Virtue is *not* its own reward."

Brynne smiled. "No, I guess not. But it *will* get better. If there's one thing I've learned, it's that time *does* heal."

"I know. I actually go for hours at a time now without thinking about Todd." Then she continued, "But enough of my soap opera. Tell me about Kirkcudbright and Castle Fraser and Ross. No, let me rephrase that—just tell me about Ross. He's the important thing. When are you two getting hitched?"

Brynne sat back on the sofa and pulled her knees up to her chin, clasping her hands around them. "We're not getting hitched. In fact, the last time I saw him, which was three weeks ago, he basically told me he'd had it with me."

"What?" Jane was stunned. "What did you do to the poor man?"

"Wait a minute. What happened to sisterly devotion? Why aren't you on my side?"

"Because I know that Ross was crazy about you. And if he walked out, it's because you did something."

"I simply refused to marry him at the precise moment he wanted to get married," Brynne explained tartly.

"Aha, I was right. You're being your usual stubborn self."

"I'm sure marriage to Ross won't be easy," Brynne insisted defensively.

"No, it will probably be downright tumultuous at times. But I'll bet it will be worth it."

Brynne sighed heavily. "Oh, hell, Jane, whoever thought love would be so complicated!"

"I know. Isn't it the pits?" Then she added, "You're older, Brynne, you know how hard life is. Why didn't you tell me?"

"I didn't want to spoil your childhood," Brynne answered dryly.

Suddenly both sisters laughed.

"Well, I have the perfect remedy," Jane said, rising and grabbing her jacket. "Chocolate éclairs at La Patisserie."

"Right. We'll eat ourselves into a stupor," Brynne agreed.

But as she followed Jane out the door, her heart was anything but light.

The next afternoon, Brynne went to the gallery. Her paintings had been shipped directly there, and only needed to be hung for the show.

Jason was his usual ebullient self, sounding reassuringly confident as he predicted that Brynne would be a big success.

Inwardly Brynne lacked Jason's confidence. She was, in fact, growing more nervous by the minute. If even one person accused her of trading on her connection with Allen, she knew it would devastate her.

That evening Brynne dressed in a white satin jumpsuit. This opening night of the show was fairly formal, but she didn't want to look like a debutante. She pulled her hair back in a tight knot at the nape of her neck. Then, as a final touch, she put on the dangly gold earrings she had worn in her role as a sophisticated gallery owner.

As she drove down San Antonio Road, she saw the ocean glistening silver and black in the moonlight. The beach stretched broad and empty. Suddenly Brynne pulled the car over to the side of the road and got out. Taking off her thin-heeled silver shoes, she tossed them on the seat, then closed the door and headed toward the beach.

She walked on the sand, feeling it cold and soft beneath her bare feet, until she came close to the water's edge. Then she sat down, crossing her ankles in front of her, and rested her chin on her knees.

All of the excitement and trepidation she felt about this show couldn't disguise the awful emptiness inside her. On this night, when her career as an artist hung in the balance, it was Ross she was thinking of.

Where is he? she wondered. *Does he miss me? Or has he put me behind him forever?*

Looking at the curve of the bay in the distance, Brynne saw a cypress tree, bent and gnarled, silhouetted against the thin, pale

November moon. Did Ross think of her when he looked at that same moon? Brynne wondered pensively.

She knew now that even if she were a success tonight, as she thought was likely, it would mean nothing if she had lost Ross. Lady Grace was right, she thought. Loneliness is a high price to pay for freedom.

At that moment she came to a decision. She would fly back to Scotland tomorrow. She would find Ross and somehow make him understand and forgive. She wouldn't make Laurie Fraser's mistake of waiting too long to go to her lover.

Rising, Brynne dusted the sand from her clothes and walked purposefully back to the car. It was time, she knew, to step out of the shadows in her life and get on with the business of loving the man who was her heart's desire.

When she arrived at the gallery, Jane was waiting for her.

"Ah, the artist as fashion plate," Jane said, smiling. Then she continued quickly, "Your paintings are terrific! Everyone loves them."

Looking around the gallery, Brynne saw people scrutinizing her paintings carefully. Several of her friends were present, but there were also strangers whom Brynne instinctively recognized as art collectors. The small gallery, with its pristine white walls covered with art, was, in fact, packed tonight. Besides the people looking at the paintings, others stood in small groups discussing art, while some people helped themselves to champagne and hors d'oeuvres from a small table in a corner.

"Brynne, here you are! We've been waiting for you."

It was Jason, and with him was a short, plump man whom Brynne immediately recognized as the art critic from the *Chronicle*.

"Have you met David Chomsky?" Jason asked.

"Yes, I have. It's nice to see you again," Brynne replied, trying to sound calm.

"We met at one of your husband's shows, I believe," Chomsky responded. "By the way, I was very sad to hear of his death. It was a tremendous loss to the art world."

"Thank you," Brynne murmured.

"I see you're painting under your maiden name," Chomsky continued.

"Yes," Brynne replied tersely. There was nothing more to add. She wasn't about to explain to Chomsky her personal reasons for dissociating herself from Allen's famous name.

"I must say, I admire that," he went on, surprising Brynne. "And I admire your work."

Jason, who'd clearly been barely able to stand quietly while Brynne and Chomsky chatted, interjected happily, "Yes, Brynne, David's told me he's going to give you a major review."

"I'd like to get an interview with you, if I may," Chomsky went on. "Jason tells me you live in Scotland now. When are you returning?"

"Tomorrow," Brynne answered.

Jane looked startled; then she smiled in understanding.

"Well, then, we'd better do the interview tonight," Chomsky said. "Why don't we go sit in that corner over there, away from the crowd."

A half-hour later, the interview was over and Chomsky had left. The moment he was gone, Jason came up to Brynne and whispered eagerly, "He'll make your reputation. I've already sold a couple of pieces tonight. When his review comes out, I'm sure they'll all sell out."

"Jason, I don't know what to say."

"Well, I do," Jane said, grinning broadly. "Where's the champagne? We've got to celebrate. And I'm not just referring to your show."

Two hours later, the preview was over and the last guest had left. Several of the pictures had "Sold" tags on them. Brynne was feeling a pleasant sense of euphoria that was only partly due to the champagne she had drunk.

"Need a lift?" Jane asked as she put on her coat before stepping out into the cold November night.

"No, I brought my car," Brynne replied. "Thanks, anyway. But I could use a lift to the airport tomorrow."

"Sure. I'll call you in the morning to arrange a time. 'Night."

When she had gone, Jason said, "There's a little champagne left. Let's sit down and finish it off. My feet are killing me."

"Okay," Brynne agreed, smiling. "Tonight

I'm in a mood to celebrate. I've settled a lot of things in my own mind."

Jason looked at her curiously, then poured a glass of champagne and handed it to her.

"You're as good, in your own way, as Allen was. That was what was worrying you, wasn't it?"

"Yes. I'm not sure I'm as good as Allen, though I appreciate your saying so. But I know I'm good enough, and I'm no longer concerned with comparisons. I'm my own person now. Before tonight, I didn't feel that way."

"I imagine that living with a certifiable genius can leave you with some deep self-doubts," Jason commented perceptively.

"Yes. It's been hard to get away from that. I felt as if I was still in Allen's shadow. But I don't feel that way now."

"Good. You've started a new life for yourself in Scotland. It's important that you not hobble it with chains from the past."

"I know. I don't intend to let that happen anymore."

Brynne looked at Jason thoughtfully as she sipped the champagne. Finally she asked, "Jason . . . why didn't you ever marry?"

He glanced at Brynne sharply, clearly surprised by the question.

"Do you mind my asking?" Brynne continued.

"No." He was silent for a long moment; then he went on, "I suppose everything in life is a matter of timing. I've been lucky. I was born into a family that was not only wealthy but also affectionate and supportive. I felt I could have whatever I wanted of life. When I was young, in my twenties, I simply had a good time. I didn't want marriage then."

"And later . . ."

"Later, the timing just wasn't right. I fell in love for the first and last time with a woman who was married. Her husband had fought in Vietnam and been crippled. She felt too much loyalty to him to leave him. She was a very exceptional person . . ."

Jason's voice trailed off and his eyes clouded with profound sadness. For the first time, Brynne saw Jason as he really was—beneath the easy charm, the light banter, the privileged life—a deeply lonely man.

He finished softly, "She was the one who found the courage to end it finally. It was tearing both of us apart. There was no other way. If only I'd met her before she married . . . Yes, timing is everything. If you miss that one right time, sometimes you never get another chance."

Brynne was silent, filled with pity for Jason, and fear for herself.

Have I missed that one right time with Ross? she wondered desperately.

"Well, I'd better lock up," Jason said, his voice heavy. "Want to go somewhere for a drink?"

"No, thanks. I've got a phone call to make," Brynne said, rising. She leaned over and kissed Jason affectionately on the cheek. "Thanks for making tonight possible."

A few minutes later she hurried into her house and quickly placed a call to Ross's apartment in Edinburgh. It was nine o'clock

A.M., Saturday, and she expected to find him at home. To her surprise, there was no answer. She tried calling Fleming House, but when the butler answered, he said Ross wasn't there and wasn't expected.

"Well, if you should speak to him, would you tell him I'll be home Sunday?" Brynne asked. "And please tell him it's very important that I talk to him."

"Very well, miss," the butler said, then rang off.

Brynne didn't know if Ross would receive the message; or, if he did, if he would even care.

Chapter Twenty-one

Brynne arrived in Kirkcudbright two days later, early in the afternoon. Her car was waiting in the small parking lot of the train station, where she had left it only a few days earlier. As she tossed her luggage in the backseat, she was both tired and worried. When her plane had landed in Glasgow that morning, she'd called Ross's apartment, but there was no answer. She then called Fleming House, but there was no answer there either. She knew that the servants were probably at church, and could only hope that Ross was also.

As she drove down the High Street, Brynne suddenly saw Donald Drummond walking along the street. Pulling up beside him, she asked anxiously, "Donald, have you seen Ross lately?"

"Why, hello, Brynne. 'Tis good to see you back. We didna' expect ye so soon." Finally answering her question, he said, "But, no, I havena' seen Ross for some time now. Three weeks or more."

"Thank you," Brynne replied, intensely disappointed. "I'm afraid I'm in rather a hurry. Say hello to Margaret for me."

"That I will," Donald responded amiably.

Brynne drove toward Fleming House. The servants would be back by now from church, and even if Ross wasn't there, at least they might be able to tell her where he was.

During the long flight from San Francisco to Glasgow, and the seemingly interminable train ride from there to Kirkcudbright, Brynne's anxiety about finding Ross had gradually turned to something close to despair. She had the awful feeling that she wouldn't be able to find him, that their love was fated to end as tragically as Laurie and Richard's had centuries earlier.

When Brynne arrived at Fleming House, the butler told her that Ross wasn't there. "But I did speak to him last night, miss, on the telephone, an' gave him your message," the man assured her.

"Did he say where he was, or if he was coming down here?" Brynne asked.

"No, miss. He hasn't been here for some time."

"Thank you," Brynne replied dejectedly as she turned and went back to her car.

As she drove off, she felt utterly bereft and alone.

When she came to the castle, it was still and

silent, obviously deserted. Brynne's heart sank. She was overwhelmed by a sense of inescapable destiny. Now she felt the agony Laurie must have felt when she realized her lover hadn't waited for her. She had come to him too late.

And then Brynne noticed a lone figure walking on a low hill behind the castle. The sun was behind him and he was no more than a dark silhouette on this crisp, bright late-autumn day. It was probably the gardener, Brynne knew. He often came on Sunday afternoons to catch up on work that he didn't complete during the week. Yet, somehow, instinctively, Brynne felt it wasn't the gardener. Slowly she started to walk up the hill toward the figure. As she got closer, she recognized the broad shoulders and easy stride.

It was Ross.

She ran then, her feet trampling the purple heather, stumbling over the steep incline. When she reached him, she was breathless. For a moment she simply stood gazing at him with all the love in the world in her golden-brown eyes.

"You waited for me," she finally said.

He smiled that heart-melting crooked smile and answered gently, "Yes. I was furious with you for a while. You demolished my pride, and I told myself, 'To hell with her, then.' But I missed you more and more each day. And when I got your message that you were coming back today . . . Well, you are looking at a man who's far too much in love to even care about the remnants of his tattered pride."

Brynne reached up and pressed her fingertips against his lips. "Hush, love. It's not you who are humbled, it's me. I love you, Ross. I'm yours completely and forever. We were meant to be."

"No more doubts?" he asked.

"No," Brynne answered softly but with an undertone of quiet certainty. "I had to find my own way back to you, through the shadows. I've done that now. And I'll never leave you again. I was so frightened of giving up my independence, of making a commitment. But now I know that if I exercise free choice in giving up some freedom, I'm not really losing anything."

"Whatever we do, there's always a sacrifice of some sort," Ross replied.

"Yes. I was afraid of being overwhelmed by you, of losing my own identity in your more powerful one. But I know who I am now, I have confidence in myself. It's odd, but just knowing that I can be totally self-sufficient makes me more willing to depend on you. Does that make sense?"

"Yes," Ross answered, smiling. "I understand that you have to have a strong sense of your own self-worth before you can truly love another person."

He pulled her against him then, his strong arms encircling her. Looking down at her, his eyes soft with love, he said, "My sweetest lass."

He kissed her with a passion that Brynne knew would never die. And in that moment when their lips touched and their arms held each other, Brynne heard a noise. It was faraway, barely audible, and sounded like a soft sigh of contentment. Brynne knew that it might be the cool autumn wind rustling through the trees. Yet somehow she didn't believe it was.

A love that had waited for centuries had finally found fulfillment.

Enjoy love and passion, larger than life!

Let new Silhouette Intimate Moments romance novels take you to the world of your dreams ...and beyond.

Try them for 15 days, free.

Our new series, Silhouette Intimate Moments, is so full of love and excitement, you won't be able to put these books down. We've developed these books for a special kind of reader—one who isn't afraid to be swept away by passion and adventure.

The characters lead thrilling lives—and their feelings are as real and intimate as yours. So you'll share all the joys and sorrows of each heroine.

Enjoy 4 books, free, for 15 days...

When you mail this coupon, we'll send you 4 Silhouette Intimate Moments novels to look over for 15 days. If you're not delighted, simply return them and owe nothing. But if you enjoy them as much as we think you will, just pay the invoice, and we'll send you 4 books each month, as soon as they are published. And there's never a charge for postage or handling!

Mail the coupon below right now. And soon you'll read novels that capture your imagination and carry you away to the world you've always dreamed of!

--- **MAIL TODAY** ---

Silhouette Dept. PCSE06
120 Brighton Road, Box 5020, Clifton, NJ 07015

Yes! I want to be swept away by passion and adventure. Please send me 4 Silhouette Intimate Moments novels each month as soon as they are published. The books are mine to keep for 15 days, free. If not delighted, I can return them and owe nothing. If I decide to keep them, I will pay the enclosed invoice. There's never a charge for convenient home delivery—no postage, handling, or any other hidden charges.

I understand there is no minimum number of books I must buy, and that I can cancel this arrangement at any time.

Name

Address

City   State   Zip

Signature   (If under 18, parent or guardian must sign.)

This offer expires March 31, 1984. Prices and terms subject to change.

Silhouette Special Edition

MORE ROMANCE FOR
A SPECIAL WAY TO RELAX
$1.95 each

2 ☐ Hastings	21 ☐ Hastings	41 ☐ Halston	60 ☐ Thorne
3 ☐ Dixon	22 ☐ Howard	42 ☐ Drummond	61 ☐ Beckman
4 ☐ Vitek	23 ☐ Charles	43 ☐ Shaw	62 ☐ Bright
5 ☐ Converse	24 ☐ Dixon	44 ☐ Eden	63 ☐ Wallace
6 ☐ Douglass	25 ☐ Hardy	45 ☐ Charles	64 ☐ Converse
7 ☐ Stanford	26 ☐ Scott	46 ☐ Howard	65 ☐ Cates
8 ☐ Halston	27 ☐ Wisdom	47 ☐ Stephens	66 ☐ Mikels
9 ☐ Baxter	28 ☐ Ripy	48 ☐ Ferrell	67 ☐ Shaw
10 ☐ Thiels	29 ☐ Bergen	49 ☐ Hastings	68 ☐ Sinclair
11 ☐ Thornton	30 ☐ Stephens	50 ☐ Browning	69 ☐ Dalton
12 ☐ Sinclair	31 ☐ Baxter	51 ☐ Trent	70 ☐ Clare
13 ☐ Beckman	32 ☐ Douglass	52 ☐ Sinclair	71 ☐ Skillern
14 ☐ Keene	33 ☐ Palmer	53 ☐ Thomas	72 ☐ Belmont
15 ☐ James	35 ☐ James	54 ☐ Hohl	73 ☐ Taylor
16 ☐ Carr	36 ☐ Dailey	55 ☐ Stanford	74 ☐ Wisdom
17 ☐ John	37 ☐ Stanford	56 ☐ Wallace	75 ☐ John
18 ☐ Hamilton	38 ☐ John	57 ☐ Thornton	76 ☐ Ripy
19 ☐ Shaw	39 ☐ Milan	58 ☐ Douglass	77 ☐ Bergen
20 ☐ Musgrave	40 ☐ Converse	59 ☐ Roberts	78 ☐ Gladstone

MORE ROMANCE FOR
A SPECIAL WAY TO RELAX

$2.25 each

79 ☐ Hastings	85 ☐ Beckman	91 ☐ Stanford	97 ☐ Shaw
80 ☐ Douglass	86 ☐ Halston	92 ☐ Hamilton	98 ☐ Hurley
81 ☐ Thornton	87 ☐ Dixon	93 ☐ Lacey	99 ☐ Dixon
82 ☐ McKenna	88 ☐ Saxon	94 ☐ Barrie	100 ☐ Roberts
83 ☐ Major	89 ☐ Meriwether	95 ☐ Doyle	101 ☐ Bergen
84 ☐ Stephens	90 ☐ Justin	96 ☐ Baxter	102 ☐ Wallace

*LOOK FOR THUNDER AT DAWN BY PATTI BECKMAN
AVAILABLE IN AUGUST AND
SUMMER COURSE IN LOVE BY CAROLE HALSTON
IN SEPTEMBER.*

SILHOUETTE SPECIAL EDITION, Department SE/2
1230 Avenue of the Americas
New York, NY 10020

Please send me the books I have checked above. I am enclosing $_____
(please add 50¢ to cover postage and handling. NYS and NYC residents
please add appropriate sales tax). Send check or money order—no cash or
C.O.D.'s please. Allow six weeks for delivery.

NAME _____

ADDRESS _____

CITY _____ STATE/ZIP _____

Silhouette Special Edition

Coming Next Month

Wild Is The Heart by Abra Taylor

Tory Allworth knew the sea was Luc Devereux's lifeblood, but the same inevitability that made the waves crash against the cliffs made Tory challenge the sea for his love.

My Loving Enemy by Pat Wallace

Once Linda had been afraid to lose herself in Judd's arms. Now, however, when it seemed the tall Texan no longer wanted her, she realized Judd's arms were the only place she wanted to be.

Fair Exchange by Tracy Sinclair

Australia had never figured in Leslie's plans until she inherited an outback ranch and came into conflict with Raider MacKenzie. At first he wanted her land . . . but then he wanted her all-too-vulnerable heart.

Never Too Late by Nancy John

Grant Kilmartin had been so busy building his construction company that he had given little thought to building relationships, until he met Natalie. They clashed professionally, but personally they were in perfect harmony.

Flower Of The Orient by Erin Ross

Lisa loved everything about Japan with one exception: Keith Brannon, the man who was pitted against her beloved uncle in business. So why was he the only man she saw in her dreams?

No Other Love by Jeanne Stephens

Their lives had taken different paths—Tyler had gone to a small West Virginia town; Kristal to Houston. But miles were nothing when Kristal learned that Tyler was hurt—and when they came together for the second time, they knew it would be forever.